DAWN AND THE OLDER BOY

"And another thing," Mum said, "we've never even met this boy. Did you know he was going to pick you up at school today?"

I shrugged. "Nope. That's just the way Travis is. He likes to do things on the spur of the moment. He's impulsive." *And fun and exciting*, I wanted to add.

"If he really liked you," Richard said, "he would make plans to see you. He'd visit you here at the house and meet the rest of your family." . . .

"Travis *does* like me," I said. "You wouldn't believe all the presents he's given me. First a necklace and hair combs, and today he bought me some earrings in town."

"I'm not so sure I like that idea," Mum said slowly. "You hardly know him, and he's showering you with presents. Something just isn't right."

Dawn thinks that Travis is the perfect boy for her, but the babysitters are worried. Travis keeps telling Dawn what to do—he's trying to change her. If he *really* liked her, he wouldn't do that, would he?

1st CHAPTER

"I don't think orange is your colour," Claudia Kishi said thoughtfully. "You're more the peaches-and-cream type, with your light skin and blonde hair."

"Mmm, I think you're right." I stared at myself in the mirror and reached for a tissue. The orange lipstick had to go. I looked as if I'd just kissed a pumpkin.

"Try this," Claudia went on, handing me a tube of gooey pink lip gloss. It reminded me of used bubble gum.

Claudia caught the expression on my face and burst out laughing. "Trust me, Dawn. It will look fantastic on you."

Claudia is an artist and can see shapes and colours in a way that nobody else can. It's a good thing that she's creative because she's not the world's best pupil. (She's a terrible speller.) And just to make things worse, she has an incredibly brainy older sister called

Janine. Janine is the type of girl who sits around doing quadratic equations for *fun*. Honest.

But back to the story. I glanced around Kristy Thomas's bedroom and saw that all six of my friends were experimenting with lipstick and nail varnish. A few of them, like Stacey McGill, were even trying out new hairstyles. It was a sort of mass "make-over", and there was a lot of giggling going on. (And some of the "befores" looked better than the "afters", if you know what I mean.)

I think I should stop right here and introduce everybody before I tell you anything else about the sleepover at Kristy's. First of all, all seven of us are members of the Babysitters Club (or BSC), which I'll explain about later. My name is Dawn Schafer, and I am the alternate officer of the club. I live in Stoneybrook, Connecticut, and I'm thirteen years old. My friends all say I *look* like a California girl with my long blonde hair and sparkly blue eyes. This makes sense since I lived in California before my parents got divorced and my mum and my brother Jeff and I moved to Stoneybrook. Now Jeff lives in California again with my father (he just wasn't happy in Connecticut), and sometimes I go back to visit. What else would you like to know? Well, I love the outdoors, I'm a vegetarian, and I try to eat a healthy diet. (Unlike

2

Claudia, who thinks Dime Bars are nature's perfect food.)

Claudia is a beautiful, dramatic-looking Japanese-American who loves exotic clothes. (She's also the vice-chairman of the BSC.) Claudia's one of those people who can wear anything and get away with it. Today, for example, she had stuck to two colours: black and white. Black cotton bib overalls over a white cotton polo neck with a shiny black patent leather belt looped around her waist. Black suede ankle boots and white cotton socks. Long black hair swept off her face with giant white plastic combs. Anyone else would look like a penguin in that get-up, but Claudia looked great.

"What do you think?" she asked, holding up a white hoop earring next to her face. "Too much?"

I nodded. "Maybe just a little." The earring was the size of a doorknob.

"Hey, Dawn, will you have a look at my hair?" asked Mary Anne. Mary Anne Spier is my stepsister (my mother married Richard, her father) and she's also my best friend. Mary Anne is a lot less daring with clothes and make-up than I am, but she has grown up quite a bit in the past year.

When I first met Mary Anne, she looked like a little girl. She was wearing little-girl clothes and, worst of all, she was wearing her brown hair in two long plaits. Awful! When I got to know her better, I realized

3

that she's really sweet and very sensitive, and that she dressed like that because her father chose all her clothes. Mary Anne's mother died when Mary Anne was just a baby, so her father has always been very protective of her. Luckily, he's loosened up a lot since he married my mum, and Mary Anne dresses like a normal thirteen-year-old now. And she even has a steady boyfriend. She's the only one of us BSC members who can say that. Her boyfriend's called Logan Bruno, and he's part of the club, too. Mary Anne is the club secretary.

"What's the problem?" I asked, rushing over to her side of the room. The minute the words were out of my mouth, I knew the answer.

Stacey McGill (a real New York girl) was busily "scrunching" Mary Anne's long brown hair into a tangled mane that trailed down her back. Very hip, very in, but not very "Mary Anne". I thought it looked fantastic, but I knew that Mary Anne wasn't happy with it. Mary Anne usually wears her hair in a smooth style; she's used to seeing herself in a certain way. (I should explain that Mary Anne would never complain to Stacey, because she doesn't like to hurt anyone's feelings.)

"Honestly, Mary Anne, if you'd just keep your hands out of the way, this would go a lot quicker." Stacey had scrunched her own hair into a cloud of blonde curls and was trying for the same effect with my stepsister.

Mary Anne shot me a desperate look in the mirror, just as Stacey gave a final pat to her hair and said pointedly, "doesn't she look great?"

I was on the spot. "I think it's a nice change," I began. "Of course, you wouldn't have to wear it like that every day."

"She should. It's a big improvement," Stacey said flatly. Stacey McGill, the club treasurer, is very fashion-conscious and always wears the newest, trendiest clothes. She's sophisticated, like Claudia (who happens to be her best friend), and she has boyfriends sometimes, but no steady ones. She's an only child and grew up in New York City until her father's company transferred him to Connecticut. The McGills had lived in Stoneybrook for a year when her father was sent *back* to New York. We all said tearful goodbyes to Stacey and wondered if we would ever see her again. About a year later, Stacey's parents got divorced, and Stacey and her mum returned to Connecticut. Talk about a complicated life! Stacey still seems like a New York girl at heart (just like I'm a California girl at heart) and she visits her father in New York whenever she can.

Just to add to Stacey's problems, she's got a severe form of diabetes. She's very careful about what she eats and knows how

5

to give herself insulin injections every day. Diabetes is something she has to live with, but at least she can keep it under control. The main thing she has to remember is not to eat sweets. Just imagine a life without sugar and sweets, and you'll get the idea. At first, we tried not to have biscuits or things lying around where she could see them, but we discovered that Stacey has a lot of self-control. She doesn't eat those things because she knows she could get really ill.

"Well, it's finished," Stacey said. She put down the brush and reached for an apple. The rest of us were munching on fudge (except for me—too unhealthy), but that's off-limits for Stacey, of course.

"I appreciate it, I really do," Mary Anne said earnestly. I knew that Mary Anne would never wear her hair that way again, but she managed to look as if she were thrilled with her new style.

"I'll be happy to do it for you anytime," Stacey said. "The thing to remember is to use just a little bit of gel and—" She stopped talking suddenly and sat down on Kristy's bed.

"Are you okay?" asked Kristy. (Kristy Thomas is the chairman of the Babysitters Club, and she's a take-charge sort of person.)

"I'm fine," Stacey said lightly. She put her hand up to her forehead, just for a second, as though she had a headache.

6

"You look a bit pale," Kristy said, peering at her. I remembered that Stacey hadn't felt well for the past few days.

"Hey, I'm fine. Really." Stacey bounced right back on her feet and picked up her hairbrush. "I think I'm a little dizzy from all the hairspray," she said with a smile. "Maybe we should get some air in here."

"Good idea." As usual, Kristy took command of the situation and marched over to the nearest window. Sometimes I get a bit annoyed because Kristy tends to be bossy (wait till you see her at a club meeting, and you'll understand), but I have to admit she really gets things done. It's funny, because in some ways, Kristy seems younger than thirteen. She has no interest in clothes and make-up and practically lives in her favourite outfit: a sweat-shirt, faded jeans, and trainers. But in other ways, she seems very mature and is exactly the kind of person you would want to have around in an emergency.

Kristy has an interesting family. She has three brothers—Sam and Charlie, who are at high school, and David Michael, who's only seven. For a long time, Mrs Thomas supported the family all by herself, because her husband had walked out one day and never come back. It was very hard on everyone, but Mrs Thomas managed to get a good job and keep the family together. Then (and this is the wonderful part) she met a millionaire called Watson Brewer and they married and the Thomases moved across town into his mansion! It sounds like something out of a film, doesn't it? Watson Brewer has two children, Karen, who's just turned seven, and Andrew, who's four, so Kristy found herself with a new brother and sister. (They only live with their father every other weekend and for two weeks during the summer, though.) Things got even *more* interesting after that because the Brewers adopted an adorable little Vietnamese girl whom they called Emily. By now Kristy's family was beginning to look like the Brady Bunch, so Nannie, Kristy's grandmother, moved in to help. Kristy loves her new family, and since she's terrific with kids, she's a big help with her younger brothers and sisters.

Okay, now I need to tell you about the two junior officers of the BSC, Mallory Pike and Jessica Ramsey. While the rest of us are eighth-graders at Stoneybrook Middle School, they are eleven and in the sixth grade at SMS. They're very different, but they're best friends.

Actually, Mal and Jessi have a couple of things in common. They're both the oldest in their families (that can have some good points and some bad points). And they share some interests.

Let's start with Mal. Mal comes from an *enormous* family. She has seven brothers and sisters, including a set of identical triplets (boys). She's very creative and loves to read and write and draw. Her ambition in life is to write and illustrate children's books, and I think she'd do a wonderful job.

Jessi has an eight-year-old sister named Becca (short for Rebecca) and a baby brother named Squirt. Squirt? That's right. His real name is John Philip Ramsey Jr., but he was so tiny when he was born that the nurses in the hospital nicknamed him Squirt.

Jessi also likes reading (she and Mal both love horse stories), but her real talent is quite different from Mallory's. Jessi wants to be a professional dancer and has studied ballet for years. It takes a lot of skill and hard work to get roles in major ballets and to perform in front of hundreds of people, but Jessi's got what it takes. She doesn't even get stage fright. (I know I'd be scared stiff if I had to do something like that.)

Another difference between Jessi and Mal—Jessi is black and Mal is white.

I have a lot more things I want to tell you about my friends (especially about my stepsister, Mary Anne, and the really romantic way our parents got together), but I'll have to save that for later. Stay tuned!

2nd CHAPTER

At eleven o'clock the following morning, Mary Anne tapped me on the shoulder.

"Dawn, wake up," she said urgently. "It's practically lunchtime!"

I snuggled deeper into my sleeping bag and buried my face in the pillow. "Uh-huh," I mumbled. What was Mary Anne getting all steamed up about? *Nobody* bounces out of bed the morning after a sleepover, and besides, we hadn't turned out the lights till three a.m. No wonder I felt like a zombie.

But Mary Anne wouldn't give up. She sat down next to me. "I think we should all get up right this minute," she said firmly. "We've already wasted half the day!"

"Stop talking," Stacey muttered from her sleeping bag. "Some people are trying to sleep."

"I know you are," Mary Anne apologized.

"But I think the Brewers expect us to turn up for breakfast. We shouldn't be lounging around in bed all morning when they're trying to feed sixteen in the kitchen." I hated to admit it, but I decided Mary Anne was probably right. I also thought that my stepsister was the only person in the whole world who would worry about something like that.

"Mmm, I think I smell bacon cooking," Mal said. She wriggled off her lilo and stretched. "I agree with Mary Anne. We should all go downstairs."

Jessi gave a gigantic yawn. I've decided to have breakfast in bed," she said sleepily. "Just leave a tray outside the door for me."

"Ha! Fat chance!" Claudia yelled, tossing a pillow at her. "If we get up, *you* get up."

Mary Anne yanked open the curtains, and the room was flooded with harsh yellow sunlight. Everybody *really* woke up after that, including Kristy, who had burrowed like a mole under her fluffy pink quilt.

"Hey, Kristy," Stacey asked, "do we have to get dressed to go down to breakfast?"

"On a Saturday morning? Are you kidding?" Kristy grinned and jammed her feet into a pair of fat down slippers. "That's the great part about weekends. You can wear whatever you like, and Mum and Watson won't care. Honest."

Claudia glanced in the mirror. Her hair was a mass of tangles and her mascara had

11

smudged over her cheekbones in two dark shadows. She looked like someone straight out of *Night of the Living Dead*.

"Claudia, you look awful," Kristy said cheerfully.

"You don't look so terrific yourself," Claudia retorted. She wasn't in the least bit offended because the truth is we *all* looked awful.

"I know. Isn't it fun?" Kristy grabbed her favourite baseball cap (the one with the collie on it) and plunked it on her head. "But who's going to see us at breakfast except for Karen and Nannie and Mum and everyone?"

A few minutes later we had our answer. Who was going to see us? Only the most gorgeous guy in the whole world!

Talk about having a panic attack. All seven of us had trooped downstairs, looking our absolute worst, when we realized there were *boys* sitting around the kitchen table! Two of them were Kristy's older brothers, Charlie and Sam, and the other looked like a film star. Sandy brown hair, deep blue eyes, and a smile that I knew I would never forget. Claudia was in front of me, and she skidded to a stop just like the Road Runner in that Saturday morning cartoon programme. Naturally, I bumped into her, and she lurched against the back of Sam's chair.

"Oh, Claudia. Hi there." He glanced at Kristy. "I figured you were going to sleep all day." Sam took a quick peek at the rest of us, and his jaw dropped open. Why hadn't we taken a few extra minutes to brush our hair and put on some make-up? (Or at least take off the old make-up?) I know I looked terrible. I have very fair skin and, as I've said, my hair is so blonde it's practically white. Can you imagine what I look like first thing in the morning, especially with mascara smudges under my eyes?

I tried to duck behind Stacey, who immediately caught on and started inching her way back towards the hallway.

"Hey, don't run away," Charlie teased her. "Kristy, I want you and your friends to meet someone." He waved a hand at the fantastic-looking boy at the table. "Travis, meet my sister and the rest of the Babysitters Club. Travis has just moved to Stoney-brook," he went on.

Travis half rose out of his chair and smiled at everyone. (He could afford to be cheerful. He looked terrific, and the rest of us were wrecks.) The other kids in the family were at the table with him. Emily was spooning up cornflakes with David Michael, Karen, and Andrew, but I barely looked at them. I couldn't take my eyes off Travis (and I couldn't stop wishing I were invisible)! Why did I have to look my absolute worst?

Travis was too polite to look shocked, though, and I thought I would drop through

13

the floor when he reached across the table and shook my hand! No one my age shakes hands (do they?), but somehow it seemed just right when Travis did it.

I could feel a little ripple of excitement go through the group, even though most of us were busily staring at our toes and wishing we were on another planet. There was this incredibly long silence while everyone waited for someone else to think of something to say, and Travis and I just stood and stared at each other.

Without thinking, I blurted out the first words that came into my head. "Is that muesli you're eating?" Not the brightest remark in the world, but you have to realize that this was a crisis situation. Think how you would feel if you happened to be wearing a tattered old nightdress and a three-sizes-too-big bathrobe at a time like this. It was enough to make anyone tongue-tied.

"That's right," Travis said easily. "It's practically the state food in California." *He was from California!* "Why don't you join us?" He gestured to an empty seat beside him, and it was all I could do not to throw myself into it. Then I remembered my shiny face (and morning breath) and decided against it.

"Oh, we'll get something to eat later," I said, trying to sound totally calm and in command of the situation. (I wasn't in control at all, and my heart was beating like a rabbit's.)

"Breakfast is the most important meal of the day," he said teasingly.

"I know that," I replied, nodding. If he wanted to talk about nutrition, that was fine with me. Mum and I are fanatics about eating healthy food, and we even make our own breakfast cereal.

Kristy, as usual, took charge. "I really think we should be heading back upstairs," she said firmly.

"Yeah, that's right." Claudia was stepping sideways towards the door.

"Without having breakfast?" Sam said, looking amused, as if he knew exactly what we were up to.

Claudia shrugged and pushed her long black hair out of her face. "Well, actually, we . . . uh, left our electric curlers switched on in the bathroom."

"Oh, that's right," Mary Anne piped up. (I should tell you that Mary Anne is a *terrible* liar.) "Gosh," she added, "if we don't get back upstairs straight away, the curlers might overheat and burn the house down." Charlie sniggered and even Travis looked amused.

Without another word, all seven of us stampeded towards the door. I had time for one last look at Travis, and when his blue eyes homed in on mine, I felt a funny little flutter in my chest.

Upstairs, I had a quick shower and spent the next hour fiddling with my hair and make-up. I decided that I wanted to look casual (but gorgeous!) and finally settled on a pale blue ten-button top with my favourite jeans. (Not that I had much choice, since I'd only packed for an overnight stay.)

When we went back downstairs it was almost twelve o'clock, and guess what? The boys were still there! I couldn't believe my luck. I made *sure* that Travis noticed me and slid onto the bench next to him.

"You must be starving," he said, pushing a bowl of fruit towards me.

"Ravenous," I replied, taking a tiny bite of an apple. Who could think about food at a time like this?

"Hey, Travis," Charlie spoke up, "have I mentioned that you and Dawn have something in common? She's from California, too."

"Really? That's fantastic." Travis looked as if he'd been waiting all his life for this bit of information. "Do you miss the ocean? We lived right on the ocean, and I used to go for long walks on the beach every night after dinner."

"You *did*? We didn't live on the ocean, but I used to go for long walks, too." I was so excited I nearly dropped my apple. Have you ever met someone and felt as if you've always known that person? That was the way I felt about Travis.

16

"There's a place just above Malibu," Travis began, "and when the sun sets, it looks as if it's dropping right into the ocean."

"I know. I went there once." I felt almost giddy. Travis and I talked non-stop for the next half hour and I have *never* met anyone whose feelings were so close to my own. We could have been twins.

"You know, you should always wear blue," Travis said, gently touching my sleeve. "It brings out the colour of your eyes. Just like the ocean. . . ."

What an unbelievable morning! I couldn't get Travis off my mind for the rest of the day, and I practically drove Mary Anne insane talking about him.

"Mary Anne, do you believe in love at first sight?" I asked her the minute we were back home.

"I think so," she said slowly. "Look at your mother and my father. I think they fell in love at first sight at high school. It's just that it took them all this time to get together."

Remember that romantic story I promised to tell you about our parents? This is it. My mum went out with Mary Anne's father at high school (we didn't know this when I first moved to Stoneybrook) and they went steady. They were madly in love with each other—but now comes the sad part. My grandparents (my mum's mother and father) disapproved of Mary Anne's father and didn't want my mum to keep seeing him. My mum comes from a wealthy family, and I suppose they always thought she would marry someone rich. I'm glad to say that the story has a happy ending. My mum and Richard *did* find each other again (with a little help from Mary Anne and me), and now they're happily married and we all live in my house.

I had to ask another question. "Mary Anne," I said, "don't you think Travis is the most gorgeous boy you've ever seen?"

"Travis?" She looked at me suspiciously. "Dawn, you're not going to get some kind of hopeless crush on him, are you?"

A hopeless crush! I was insulted. "Of course not," I said stiffly. "I just think he's very . . . attractive."

"Oh, well, yes," Mary Anne said. "I do, too. Of course, *I* think *Logan* is gorgeous." She paused. We know each other so well that she could read my mind. "Dawn," she said, "He's at *high* school. . . !"

"I know that."

"And even if *you* like *him*, it doesn't mean he's going to ask you out or anything."

"Right." I changed the subject then, but my mind kept racing along the same channels. I had found the one boy in the world for me, and his name was Travis.

3rd
CHAPTER

A lot of kids hate Mondays, but I don't mind them. Why? Because Monday is the first meeting of the week for the Babysitters Club. I know you're probably wondering about the club and how it works, so I'm going to fill you in on our last meeting. It took place the Monday after the sleepover, and if you're guessing that I was still thinking about Travis, you're absolutely right.

I should begin by telling you that we meet on Mondays, Wednesdays, and Fridays, and that we start *promptly* at five-thirty. And that means on the dot! Kristy Thomas, our chairman, is a stickler for being on time (and for a lot of other rules as well). We meet for half an hour, until six o'clock.

I rushed into Claudia's bedroom about two minutes late (due to a sitting job), and got an icy glare from Kristy. She was sitting in her director's chair, as usual, and made a big drama out of looking at Claud's digital clock, the official BSC timekeeper. She didn't say anything, but she gave her head a little shake, and I knew she was annoyed.

"Sorry," I said, stepping between Mallory and Jessi, and setting myself on Claud's bed between Claud and Mary Anne. Mal and Jessi were smiling at each other, and I knew that they were trying not to giggle at some private joke. Since they're a couple of years younger than the rest of us, you'd think that Kristy would bend the rules a little for them. No way! Whoever said rules are made to be broken has never met Kristy Thomas.

You're probably curious about why we meet in Claudia's bedroom. That's easy—Claudia is the only one of us with her own phone and personal phone number. And a phone is very important when you're running an organization like the BSC. Why did I call it an organization? Because it's partly a club and partly a business.

Maybe I'd better slow down and tell you how it all started. One day, before Kristy's mother had married Watson, when Kristy still lived opposite Claudia and next door to Mary Anne, she noticed that her mother was phoning all over town, trying to find a babysitter for David Michael, Kristy's little brother. Kristy had a brainwave. Why not form a babysitters club—an organization that parents could phone to reach several sitters at once.

This is the way our club works. My friends and I meet three times a week, as I've mentioned, and anyone who wants a babysitter can phone us at those times—and reach *seven* sitters. It's wonderful for the parents and great for us. We sometimes have more jobs than we can handle (which is why we have a couple of backup babysitters), and everything is done on a very professional basis.

We have elected officers, we collect subs money, and we keep very accurate records of who sits when and how much money they make. We also write down our babysitting "experiences" in a notebook. This information is very helpful to all the club members and gives us tips about what to expect from the kids.

You already know that Kristy Thomas is the chairman, and I'd say that she is perfect for the job. Even though she does tend to be a little bit bossy, I have to admit that she keeps the club running well. (Also, let's face it. I can't really think of anyone else in the club who would want to be chairman. It's a *lot* of responsibility. Besides, the club was Kristy's idea.)

Claudia Kishi is our vice-chairman. We felt it was only fair since we use her room three times a week, use her phone, and eat her junk food.

Mary Anne is the secretary, and she looks after the record book. Don't get confused. The record book is different from the notebook. The record book is like a giant appointment book. Mary Anne schedules every single babysitting job, and since she's very good at details, she actually *enjoys* doing this. She also keeps track of clients' names, addresses, and phone numbers, and the rates our clients pay. Mary Anne could tell you anything about our schedules—the date of Jessi's next dance class, or when Mal is due to have her brace checked at the dentist's. She *never* makes mistakes, and as far as I know, has never mixed up a baby-sitting appointment. That job would drive me straight up the wall, but Mary Anne loves it.

Stacey McGill is the club treasurer because she's practically a genius with numbers. She keeps track of who makes what (each of us keeps the money we make, though; we don't split it with the group), but it's good to know how things stand. Stacey is also responsible for collecting subs from everyone each Monday. The subs are pretty low, and the money is well spent, but it's still hard to get people to part with money. Actually, the subs are important for several reasons. We help Claudia pay her phone bill, and we pay Charlie, Kristy's older brother, to drive her to and from the meetings, since she lives in a different

22

neighbourhood, now that her mother has married Watson. We also use the money to restock our Kid-Kits (I'll explain later), and if there's any money left over, we blow it on fun things like pizza parties.

Not to be snide or anything, but as alternate officer, I think I have the most interesting job in the BSC. I get to fill in for any club member who can't attend a meeting. Since Kristy is such a stickler for attendance, that hardly ever happens, but I've been the vice-chairman and the secretary, and I was club treasurer while Stacey was back in New York. I like being able to try all different jobs.

Mal and Jessi are our junior officers because they're not allowed to babysit at night yet, unless it's for their own brothers and sisters. Still, they're both *very* responsible and are a big help to us in the club by taking on a lot of the after-school jobs.

Finally, we have two associate members, Shannon Kilbourne and Logan Bruno— Mary Anne's boyfriend! Shannon and Logan don't come to our regular meetings, but we know we can call on them in a crisis when we really get swamped with jobs. They're both good babysitters.

Anyway, back to the meeting. We were discussing club business, but my mind was filled with Travis. I was *dying* to ask Kristy if she'd seen him again, but I couldn't think

of any way of slipping it into the conversation.

Kristy must have noticed that I was a
million miles away because she suddenly
said, "How about you, Dawn? Do you need
some more crayons or Magic Markers for
your Kid-Kit?"

It took me a minute to come back to earth.
"Uh, no, but I'd like to buy a few more
colouring books."

This is what a Kid-Kit is. We've each
made our own. It's a decorated cardboard
box filled with our old toys, books, and
games, and we take it with us when we
babysit. The kids love them, and the kits are
part of what makes our club so special. For
some reason, someone else's old toys are
much more interesting than your own.
However, although the toys and games last
forever, certain items, like crayons and
colouring books, need to be replaced from
time to time. We use money from the
treasury for this.

My mind was racing, though, trying to fit
Travis into the conversation, and a minute
later, I got my chance. Kristy mentioned
that Charlie would be a bit late picking her
up at Claudia's.

"Oh, really? Is he out somewhere with
Travis?" I asked, trying to sound ultra-
casual.

Kristy gave me a funny look. "No, he's at
the dentist having a filling done."

"Oh, that doesn't sound like much fun." I tried to laugh, but it didn't quite come off. "So how's he doing, anyway?" I asked.

Kristy rolled her eyes. "I'm sure he's fine. It was a very small filling. Now if we can get back to business . . ."

"I don't mean Charlie," I said quickly. "I mean Travis." *Everybody* was looking at me now, and I knew I was probably giving the whole thing away by being so persistent.

Kristy shrugged. "How should I know?" She glanced down at the notebook, all set to talk about Charlotte Johanssen, who is one of our favourite sitting charges.

"You mean Travis hasn't been back to your house?" The words just tumbled out.

Kristy looked at me suspiciously. "Maybe once or twice," she said vaguely. "I think he came over to play basketball yesterday."

"You *think*?" How could she not know a thing like that?

"There were a lot of boys playing basketball in the drive," she snapped. "Now we really need to . . ."

I blocked out the rest of what Kristy was saying. Item one: Travis may or may not have been back to her house. Item two: Travis *probably* hadn't mentioned me, at least not to Kristy. (But maybe to one of her brothers? I couldn't be sure.) I really hadn't found out very much in this conversation, but at least it was fun to talk about Travis. I just liked hearing his name!

The phone rang just then, and Kristy grabbed it. "Good afternoon, Babysitters Club." Kristy listened for a few moments, jotted down some notes, and promised to get back to the caller. I should explain that everyone is "equal" in our club. Just because you answer the phone doesn't mean you can take the job for yourself (although this has happened a few times). Instead, you are supposed to write down the details of the job, discuss it with the club members, let Mary Anne check the record book, and *then* call the client back. It's a good system.

"That was Mrs Hobart," Kristy said, looking round the group. "She needs a sitter for Johnny, Mathew, and James next Saturday because Ben is taking Mal to the cinema."

Six of us gasped, and Mal turned an interesting shade of pink.

"Is that true?" I asked. "You and Ben are going out together?" I should mention that the Hobarts are an Australian family who moved into Mary Anne's old house across the street. There are four boys in the family, all with reddish-gold hair and "Aussie" accents. Ben Hobart, the oldest in the family, is Mal's age and a really nice boy.

"I wouldn't call it going out together," Mal said. She looked a little flustered, and I knew she wasn't thrilled at being the centre of attention. "We're just going to see a film."

"Sounds like going out to me," I teased her. Naturally, my mind went to Travis. I'd give *anything* to go to see a film with him, and I wouldn't care if anyone called it going out or not.

"Let's get back to business," Kristy said crisply. "Who's available on Saturday?" Mary Anne pored through the record book, and it turned out that Jessi was free.

She nodded to Kristy, who already had her hand on the phone. "Tell her I'll be there," Jessi piped up. "The Hobarts are great."

The meeting broke up shortly after that, and Mary Anne and I cycled home in the fading sunlight. I couldn't help but think about Mal and her date-that-wasn't-really-a-date. I tried to imagine what it would be like to go out with Travis. What if he just phoned me up out of the blue and asked me out? What if he asked me out for pizza or a film? What would I do, what would I say, what would I wear? I was thinking so hard, I nearly rode into the gutter.

"Dawn, wake up!" Mary Anne said. "You're in another world."

I tightened my grip on the handlebars and tried to look serious. It was hard, though, because I really *was* in another world. A world filled with just two people—myself and Travis.

4th
CHAPTER

Have you ever had a funny feeling that something exciting is going to happen to you? That's how I felt during the next few days, except I wasn't sure if it was going to be wonderful-exciting or awful-exciting. (Once I just *knew* that I was going to have an exciting day, and that was the day Claudia broke her leg. So it's better not to get your hopes up too high when that feeling hits you.)

The feeling was pretty strong by the weekend, though. At about ten o'clock on a sunny Saturday morning, Mary Anne and I were raking the leaves in the front garden while our parents were out shopping. We have a really *enormous* lawn, and when it's covered with leaves, it seems as big as a football field. But before you picture the garden, I'd better tell you about our house. When Mum and I moved to Stoneybrook after the divorce, we didn't buy an ordinary house like most people. Instead, we bought a colonial farmhouse that's over *two hundred* years old. I love it. It has lots of little rooms, and the doorways are so low that tall people have to duck under them. Mum says people used to be shorter in the 1700s. Anyway, it also has a smokehouse, a barn, and an *outhouse*. If you like spooky old houses, then you'd love this one, because it's even got a secret passage. There's a long dark tunnel that leads from my bedroom to the barn, and we think that it was probably part of the Underground Railroad, which helped slaves escape from the South before and during the Civil War. It's exactly like something out of a ghost story. (I'm a big fan of ghost stories, in case you hadn't guessed.)

But back to that Saturday morning. Mary Anne and I had got up early and pulled on our oldest jeans, ready to tackle the front garden. Even with two people raking, it was like attacking an iceberg with a toothpick, but we were making some progress. I was wearing my Walkman, lost in my own world, when Mary Anne grabbed me by the arm.

"Look, look!" she mouthed. She pushed me around so I faced the drive, and my stomach did a somersault. A dark blue Chevy was pulling up in front of our house, and a moment later, a terrific-looking boy got out. Not just *any* terrific-looking boy, though. *Travis.*

"Ohmigosh!" I whispered to Mary Anne, pulling off my headphones. "What am I going to do?" I felt as if someone had just yanked the lawn out from under my feet, and I nearly dropped the rake.

"You're going to say hello to him," Mary Anne said calmly. (It was easy for her to be calm, because she didn't feel the same way about him that I did.)

By now, Travis was strolling towards us, and without thinking, I brushed my hair out of my eyes. Unfortunately, I also left a big black smudge on my face, but I didn't realize it.

"What will I say? How do I look?" I asked desperately. Mary Anne smiled and didn't answer me. She was already waving hello to Travis and heading back towards the house. I know she was giving us the chance to talk privately (Mary Anne is *always* tactful), but suddenly, I didn't want her to leave. I was afraid to be alone with Travis, afraid that I would make an idiot out of myself. (Also, Richard and my mum have very strict rules about us having boys over when they're not at home. Boys are not allowed in the house. Full stop.)

"Hi, there," Travis said, walking up to me. (He certainly wasn't nervous.) He looked fantastic in a pair of jeans faded to just the right blue-white shade, and a heavy, new SHS (Stoneybrook High School) jacket.

"I didn't know you could drive," I blurted out. What a brilliant remark. For some reason, whenever I was with Travis, I seemed to lose the power of reasonable speech.

He shrugged, not the least bit embarrassed. "I've been driving since the day I turned sixteen."

I should explain that it's legal to drive at sixteen in Connecticut, but I don't know anyone who really starts driving at that age. Charlie Thomas' parents, and a lot of others I know, make their kids wait until they're *seventeen* before they can drive alone. Some parents even make their kids wait until they're seventeen just to take the driving test.

"Um, I like your car." This wasn't the world's most fascinating remark, either, but it was the best I could do under the circumstances.

"Thanks." Travis looked pleased, and we automatically started walking back towards the house. I waited about fifteen seconds for him to say something (it seemed like fifteen hours) and finally asked him if he'd like some lemonade.

"Maybe later," he said, turning on that thousand-kilowatt smile. "Why don't we sit out here and talk for a while." He touched my elbow and gestured to the front step.

"Sure." I gulped. So Travis really *had* come over just to talk to me. You're probably wondering why I didn't know this all along. I suppose I did, but I couldn't believe it. I nearly asked him what he wanted to talk about but caught myself just in time. I decided it was time to stop making stupid remarks and try to start a real conversation. Before I had a chance to open my mouth again, he beat me to it.

"Fifty thousand miles on her, but you'd never know it," he said, pointing to the Chevy.

I nodded, not sure how to respond. Was fifty thousand miles good or bad? It sounded like a *lot* of miles, but as I don't drive, I'm not really up on things like this. I decided to play it safe. "It's good that your parents let you borrow it," I said.

Travis laughed. "Borrow it? She's all mine. I can drive her whenever I want." He paused and pulled out a packet of sugar-free chewing gum. After offering me a stick (I refused—the last thing I wanted to do was get gum stuck to my teeth during an important conservation) he went on. "I have to pay for the petrol and the insurance."

I nodded again. I was beginning to feel like one of those doll heads that bob up and down in the back windows of cars. "It looks very . . . shiny," I said finally.

Travis beamed and I knew I'd said the right thing. "Three coats of Super-Gloss," he said proudly. "You see, Dawn, the whole trick is to dry the car thoroughly in between each coat. A lot of people don't take the time, and that's why they get water spots."

"Oh," I said appreciatively. I had never thought about water spots before, but Travis made them sound almost interesting. "I'll have to remember that."

"And always use an old terry cloth towel. It doesn't scratch the finish, but it gives you a nice shine. That's extremely important." I smiled and tried to look encouraging.

We could probably have talked about cars a little more, but Travis abruptly changed the subject. "So tell me, how do you like Stoneybrook Middle School?"

"Oh, I think it's great," I began. "All my friends are there—"

"That's nice," he cut in. "I make friends easily, too. A lot of people think it's hard to change schools, but not for me. I make friends wherever I go."

"So do you like Stoneybrook High—"

"You bet!" Travis said enthusiastically. "The first day I was there, I was invited to join five clubs. Five!" He ticked them off on his fingers. "The debating club, the drama club, the pep club, the computer club . . . oh, yeah, and the Latin club."

"That's nice," I said weakly. The Latin club didn't surprise me a bit—I was pretty sure it was all girls.

"And once they found out I play football and tennis" (Travis shook his head in mock amazement) "they drafted me on the spot."

"Wow!" That was all I could manage before Travis revved up again. I had never met anyone so energetic. (Or so talented, or so good–looking . . .)

"It was really funny," he added, "but the next day, Coach Higgins and Coach Reilly both turned up at the same time. One wanted me for basketball and the other wanted me for football." He laughed. "It was like a tug-of-war."

"I can imagine." I laughed a little to show I was getting into the spirit of things.

"Well, that's enough about me," he said suddenly. "Let's talk about you." He pulled out a small white box. "I've brought you something."

A present? I nearly fainted. Even my daydreams hadn't prepared me for this. "What is it?" I cried.

"Open it up and see." Travis grinned at me. "I think you're going to like it."

My first present from Travis. My hands were shaking as I untied the bow. "A necklace!" I lifted a string of beautiful blue beads out of the box.

"There's more," Travis said. I found two hair combs nestled in the tissue paper. They were deep blue, like the beads.

"But it's not my birthday or anything," I protested.

Travis leaned forward and gently lowered the necklace over my head. "When I saw this, it just made me think of you. That's all. It's the same shade as your eyes."

"It is?" I felt ridiculously pleased.

"Definitely. And I had a special reason for buying the combs. I saw a girl on TV who had her hair swept back at the sides, like this." He lifted my fine blonde hair and tucked it behind my ears. "This is a much better style for you. It brings out the colour of your eyes and your cheekbones. I think you should try it."

"I suppose I could," I said, flustered. "Usually, I just brush my hair and wear it straight. It's so long."

"Oh, yeah. That's another thing I wanted to mention." Travis picked up a strand of hair and looked at it critically. "When's the last time you got your hair cut?"

"Cut? I never get it cut. Well, sometimes I have the ends trimmed a little."

Travis gave me a very serious look. "I think you should lose a few inches, maybe three or four. It will give your hair more lift, you know?"

"Maybe," I said doubtfully. I like my hair the way it is—very long and fine. Whenever I try a new style, I usually hate it and just go back to wearing it straight.

"I'm not talking about anything drastic," Travis went on, "just a sort of trim. You could ask the hairdresser or someone to shape it up if you want." He laid his hand very gently over mine, just for second.

"Think about it, okay? For me."

For me! I nearly slid off the step. I knew that Travis must be really interested in me or he never would have gone to all this trouble.

"Of course I will," I told him.

He grinned and stood up. "I've got to run. My mum wants me to go shopping for her."

"Thanks for the necklace and the combs—" I began awkwardly.

"That's okay," Travis interrupted, heading towards the car. "But remember, I want to see you in that new hairstyle." He started the engine, waved goodbye, and headed down the street.

I stood rooted to the spot with a silly grin on my face. Travis liked me!

I could have stood there daydreaming forever, but I didn't want to waste a minute. I picked up the combs and dashed inside the house.

"Mary Anne!" I yelled, thundering up the stairs. "Get a brush and some scissors. We've got work to do!"

5th CHAPTER

Saturday

I never know what to expect when I sit for the Hobarts, and this time I got an even bigger surprise than usual. The kids asked me to watch them rehearse a play! And guess what. James, who is only eight years old, wrote it all by himself. He made sure that everybody got a part, and Chewy, believe it or not, was the star! It was great! I'll tell you more about it at our next meeting.

Jessi's babysitting job with the Hobarts turned out to be one of the best afternoons of her life. Who would think that putting on a play with five kids (the three Hobart boys and two of the Perkins girls) could be so much fun?

When the Hobarts first moved into the neighbourhood, naturally everyone was very curious about them. Some of the kids said that the Hobarts talked just like Crocodile Dundee, so we decided to see for ourselves. What did we find? Four boys, all with red hair and great accents! But a few kids actually *made fun* of the way the Hobarts talked, and we thought this was incredibly rude. After all, maybe the Hobarts thought *we* sounded funny with our American accents.

But back to Jessi's babysitting job. Mrs Hobart asked her to come over at two o'clock on Saturday afternoon. She and her husband were going out shopping and they needed someone to watch the three youngest boys, James, aged eight; Mathew, aged six; and Johnny, who's only four. Ben, the oldest boy, is in my class, so he obviously didn't need a sitter. And anyway, he was taking Mal to the cinema that afternoon.

The three younger boys were playing outside when Myriah and Gabbie Perkins ran over to say hello.

"Hi, Jessi Ramsey," Gabbie yelled. Gabbie is two and a half and calls most people by their full names. She's got two sisters, Myriah, who's almost six, and Laura, who's just a baby. The Perkinses moved into Bradford Court when they bought Kristy's old house. They have given the BSC lots of business, and we love to sit for them.

All three girls are great, and Myriah is especially theatrical. She can sing and dance (tap *and* ballet), and is even into gymnastics. Since Jessi is a dancer, she feels that she's got a lot in common with her. Jessi says she's always impressed when little kids can get up and perform, because she knows how hard it is to face an audience. Myriah can sing "On the Good Ship Lollipop," and she knows "Tomorrow" from *Annie* by heart. A lot of kids love to sing, but Myriah's really good at it. She's just like someone you'd see on TV. When she sings, she knows every word. She's right on pitch and she even gets the timing right.

Anyway, when the Perkins girls ran over, they didn't come alone. They brought their dog with them. Chewbacca is a huge black Labrador who's extremely friendly. (Sometimes *too* friendly!) He looks like a small bear but acts like a puppy.

"Chewbacca, stop that!" Myriah shouted. Chewbacca was running in circles, trampling the Hobarts' flower beds. "He's just had a bath," she explained, "and that always makes him crazy."

39

"Bring him over to the patio," Jessi said. "Let's all sit at the picnic table and play a game."

"What kind of game?" Mathew asked. He still has a trace of an Australian accent. "Something fun?"

"Definitely something fun." Jessi looked at Chewbacca. Playing Frisbee was out. Chewbacca had already chomped his way through three of them.

"Let's have a rehearsal," Myriah suggested. "That's my favourite thing to do in the whole world."

"A rehearsal?" Jessi said blankly. "I was thinking of playing 'I Packed My Grandmother's Trunk'—" She was immediately out-voted.

"No, we want to rehearse!" James and Mathew yelled. "We'll show you our play." I should tell you that the Hobart kids are very interested in drama, and Mathew was given the lead in his school play.

"You're putting on a play?" Jessi asked.

"An original one," James said proudly. "I'm writing it."

An eight-year-old kid writing a play? Jessi was impressed.

"We've been working on it for a couple of weeks," Myriah piped up. "Do you want to see how far we've got?"

"Of course," Jessi told her. And she saw the perfect opportunity to send Chewbacca back to his own house. "But don't you think you'd better take Chewy home first? You could leave him on the porch so he won't interrupt the rehearsal."

"No, Chewbacca has to stay," Myriah replied. "Mummy says we have to keep him outside till he dries off." She grinned. "Besides, he's our star."

Oh, no. Jessi groaned inwardly. Then she poured herself a glass of lemonade and sat back to watch the show. After a few minutes, she found herself getting *really* interested. Even though there was a lot of giggling (and almost everyone forgot some of their lines), the play was good.

The story was very simple. Chewy (the hero) was a lost dog who wandered up and down a busy shopping centre, looking for his owner. Jessi started to point out that dogs aren't usually allowed in shopping centres, but she knew that would spoil the fun.

Myriah had the opening lines. "Hello, doggie," she said abruptly. "Don't you have a home?" She walked up to Chewy and pretended to inspect his neck. "Uh-oh," she said, making a face. "No collar." She rolled her eyes. "Now it's going to be really hard to find your owner." Chewy jumped up and started licking her face. "Down, Chewy," she said sharply. "I mean, down, doggie."

Gabbie cleared her throat, eager to get in on the act. Myriah nodded and started walking across the patio with the dog. "Let's see if any of the people who work in the shopping centre know your owner," she said. "We'll start with the shoe shop."

"Want some shoes?" Gabbie asked. "We've got all kinds—yellow, green, and red. And all sizes."

Myriah stopped so suddenly that Chewy stumbled into her. "Not today, thanks," she said very seriously. "I've got a problem. This is a lost dog, and I'm looking for his owner."

"How about some shoes?" Gabbie persisted.

"Hey, Gabbie," James cried. "You're supposed to talk about the dog, not the shoes."

Myriah frowned. "Think hard," she said to Gabbie. "Have you seen his owner?"

"We've got trainers," Gabbie continued. "And cowboys boots—"

Myriah sighed. Gabbie must have forgotten the script. Myriah would just have to make the best of it. "Let's go, doggie," said Myriah. "Maybe your owner stopped off for a slice of pizza." She walked over to the barbecue grill, where Mathew was pretending to throw pizza dough in the air. "Excuse me . . ."

"Not while I'm making the dough," Mathew said. "I can't talk until I get this in the oven."

Myriah looked annoyed. It was obvious

that Mathew was adding some new lines to his script. "Look," she said, "this is an emergency."

Mathew shook his head and refused to look at her. He twirled the imaginary dough in his hand, pretending to toss it high in the sky. Finally he spread some pretend-pizza sauce on it and put it in the oven. Then he wiped his hands on a pretend-apron (a nice touch, Jessi thought) and grinned. "Okay, what do you want?"

Myriah repeated the story about the lost dog while Mathew listened intently. "Afraid I can't help you," he said, twirling another piece of dough.

Jessi was beginning to wonder what Myriah would do next when Zach came tearing round the corner on his bicycle. Zach's a good friend of James, but he's very bossy and is always telling James what to do.

When he saw Myriah leading Chewy around the patio, he came to a stop. "What are you doing?"

"We're rehearsing a play," Myriah said.

"Can I watch?"

"I suppose so," she replied. She waited until Zach had settled himself on a huge tyre, suspended from a rope, and then went on with the play. She had just taken Chewy into a department store, when Zach burst out laughing.

"This is the silliest play I've ever seen," he hooted.

"It is not," James said angrily. "I wrote it."

"You *wrote* it?" Zach laughed so hard, he nearly fell off the swing. "It's terrible!" He jumped off the tyre and headed for his bike. "And what are you doing playing with *girls*, anyway?"

"They're part of the play," James began, his face a bright red.

"I don't believe this," Zachary said, still chuckling. "First you hang around with that retard, Susan Felder, and now you're playing with a group of little kids." (Susan Felder is a handicapped girl whose family lives in the neighbourhood. She goes to a special school, doesn't talk, and doesn't know how to play with other kids.)

Jessi thought it was really mean of Zach to call her a retard and said so.

"Yeah, well, she is," Zach said bluntly. He wasn't even embarrassed. "You know something, James?" he said, swinging onto his bike. "If you really want to be an American, you've got to change. You need to hang around with me and the other boys. You need to spend more time on your skateboard. And you should dump these girls. Oh, yeah. One more thing. Stop calling your mother 'Mummy'."

James just stood there listening, his hands clenched at his sides. Finally he spoke up. "You know what your problem is, Zach?" he said very quietly. "You're just

44

jealous because you're not in the play."

"He probably can't even act," Mathew said, and Jessi giggled.

"I can so!" Zach said hotly. "Maybe I just don't want to hang around with a load of girls!" Zach pedalled as fast as he could down the drive, chanting, "James is a gi-irl, James is a gi-irl!"

James's face fell, and Jessi felt sorry for him.

Nobody said anything for a moment, and then Chewy barked. "I think he's trying to tell us it's time to go back to the play," James said. Everybody laughed. James clapped his hands loudly. "Okay, places everyone. Let's take it from the top."

Jessi felt very proud of him.

6th CHAPTER

Last Tuesday I got the biggest shock of my life! You're going to really be surprised when I tell you about it.

School had just finished, and Stacey and I had walked Kristy to her bus. Claudia and Mary Anne were trailing behind us, and everyone was trying to decide what to do next.

"Why don't you come over to my house?" Claudia offered. "Mum's bought a gallon of Pecan Crunch ice cream." She glanced at Stacey. "And there's homemade applesauce, too. The kind with no sugar."

Stacey smiled. "It sounds good, but I've got an English test tomorrow. So have you, Claudia," she added teasingly. "In case you've forgotten."

Claudia groaned and clutched her head in her hands. "You had to remind me!" She turned to me. "How about you, Dawn?"

46

I shrugged. I never eat ice cream (I like frozen yoghurt better) but I didn't want to sound rude. I was just about to make up some excuse not to go to Claudia's when a car horn tooted behind me. I turned automatically and saw—Travis!

"Ohmigosh!" I muttered under my breath.

Mary Anne spotted him at the same time. "Isn't that—"

"Yes, yes," I said quickly, practically fainting on the spot.

"Look, he's pulling over to the kerb," Stacey said, grabbing my arm. "And he's waving to you."

My mind went blank. What was Travis doing here? Did he really want to see me?

"Go over to the car," Stacey whispered, giving me a little shove. "What are you waiting for?"

What *was* I waiting for? The best-looking boy I'd ever seen in my whole life was offering me a lift, and I was frozen like a statue! I probably would have stood there forever, except that Stacey jabbed me with her spiral notebook.

"Move!" she ordered.

Travis had already pushed the passenger door open and was flashing his gorgeous smile at me.

"Hop in," he said casually. "Are you on your way home?"

"Yes, but —"

"I've got a better idea," he cut in smoothly. "How'd you like to go shopping with me? I've got to choose a birthday present for my dad."

I hesitated. Going *anywhere* with Travis would be fantastic, but I knew I should check with Mum first. I shifted from one foot to the other, trying to stall for time. Maybe I could duck back into school and phone her first? But then Travis would think I was a baby! Besides, Mary Anne could always tell Mum and Richard where I was—if she absolutely had to.

Another horn beeped, and Travis patted the front seat of his car. "C'mon," he said urgently. "This is a no-parking zone."

I made up my mind. I dumped my books on the front seat, slid inside, and a minute later we were zipping down the street, with the sounds of hard rock filling the car.

Travis waited till we stopped at a red light to turn to me. "I'm glad you decided to come," he said simply.

I grinned, relaxing a little. "So am I. There's just one thing I should warn you about. I've got to be home by six."

"No problem. We've got plenty of time. I thought we'd hit Surf and Sail first, and then we'll play it by ear." The lights changed and he turned left.

"Surf and Sail?" I repeated.

"It's a sports shop. My dad has had his eye on a new compass for a long time,

48

and they're in the sale this week."

I nodded, happy to be with him. He looked terrific in a blue cotton workshirt and faded jeans. I could hardly *believe* my good luck.

As soon as we stepped into Surf and Sail I knew I was out of my depth. I've been sailing plenty of times, but I don't know a lot about serious boating equipment. Travis stopped in front of a display case filled with compasses, and I decided to speak up. "Travis, I'm afraid I'm not going to be much help to you. Are you *sure* your father wants a compass?"

Travis laughed and slid his arm around me. "I just wanted an excuse to see you today."

"Really?" I felt a little light-headed. Travis chose a compass very quickly, and we were back on the pavement a few minutes later. Now what? I wondered. I was totally confused. (And a little disappointed. I'd been hoping that Travis would take a long time to make up his mind, so we could spend more time together.)

I started for the car, but he grabbed my elbow and steered me towards Burger Bite. "Aren't we going back home?" I asked.

"We've got hours ahead of us. I thought we'd stop for a snack and then do some more shopping."

I've got to tell you that Burger Bite is not my favourite kind of restaurant, and I was surprised that Travis wanted to go there, too, since he'd said once that he likes health food. Still, I was glad to be sitting in a back booth with him. I reached for a menu, but Travis closed his hand over mine. "We don't need that. I come in here all the time."

But I don't, I longed to say. Travis was obviously planning on ordering for me. I know some girls like it when a boy takes charge like that, but *I* like to make up my own mind. Besides, how could Travis possibly know what I felt like eating?

I practically held my breath when the waitress appeared, and wondered if I should mention that I don't eat meat. I lost my nerve at the last minute, but luckily, Travis ordered grilled cheese sandwiches for both of us.

"So," Travis said when the waitress had left. "What's been happening with you today?"

"Not much, how about you?" I still felt a bit tongue-tied with Travis and decided it was easier to let him keep the conversation going. He *always* seemed to have something to talk about.

"I tried out for track today," he said earnestly. "You wouldn't believe what happened. I was the first guy the coach picked. I suppose all that running I did in California paid off . . ." I let Travis's words drift over me, thinking how wonderful it was to be sitting there with him. If I had to describe the ideal boy, it would be Travis. Tall, good-looking, with a fantastic smile and a great personality. And he liked *me* even though he was three years older than I was.

When the sandwiches arrived a few minutes later, he had moved on to another topic, football. "You see, Coach Larson was demonstrating an intricate play for us," he said, looking into my eyes. He took a bite of sandwich and moved a salt shaker next to the napkin holder. "The quarterback ran down to the twenty-yard line like this . . ." I watched, caught up in the sound of his voice. "And then the tight end zigzagged over here . . ." He picked up a ketchup bottle and plonked it down next to the sugar bowl. "Bingo! Right over the line for a touchdown."

"That's amazing," I said, trying to look impressed.

"And you know what?" he added, sliding the pepper shaker across the table. "I was the only one there who knew what he was talking about."

"That's wonderful. You really know a lot about football."

Travis grinned. "What can I tell you?" He wolfed down the rest of his sandwich and I hurried to keep up with him.

It was almost four by the time we left Burger Bite, and I was starting to feel a little edgy. I knew Mum wouldn't be too pleased if she found out that I'd spent the afternoon with Travis (but I also knew that she and Richard wouldn't get home for another two hours). So I was safe, at least for the moment.

We walked around in town, and Travis surprised me (as usual) by leading me to the jewellery shop. "I saw some pierced ear-rings in here that would look great on you," he said. He led me to a display counter and spun an earring tree with his thumb. "Good! They're still here." He lifted a pair of delicate silver earrings off the tree and held them out to me. "Do you like them?"

They were perfect. Tiny butterflies in flight. "I love them," I said softly.

Travis held them up to my ear and smiled. "I knew they'd be right for you."

"I'll wear them under the stars," I promised him. (I should explain that I wear two earrings in each ear.)

"No," Travis said flatly. "You should wear them up higher. Just get another hole pierced in your ear."

"Three holes? I don't know," I said doubtfully. I remembered that I'd had to persuade Mum to let me get my ears pierced in the first place.

Travis laughed. "It's no big deal. All the girls in California wear them that way. It would look really cool on you."

"I'll have to think about it," I said, trying to sound casual.

"There's nothing to it," Travis answered. We were standing side by side at the cash desk. "They could probably do it for you now."

"No!" I was starting to feel a little panicky. I could just imagine Mum's reaction if I did something like that without asking her.

I felt relieved when we left the jewellery shop a few minutes later and headed back to the car, even though I knew that Travis was a tiny bit annoyed with me.

"Thanks for the earrings," I told him, trying to smooth things over.

"I'm glad you like them." He squeezed my arm. I knew I would never, *ever* forget this moment.

My happiness didn't last long though, because when I got home I had the surprise of my life. Mum and Richard were waiting for me in the kitchen.

"You're home early," I said casually, tossing my books on the kitchen table.

"You're home late," Mum answered, frowning a little. She was cutting up vegetables for a salad.

"Um, not really." I nibbled on a carrot, stalling for time. I could tell that Mum and Richard were *both* annoyed with me. What an ending to a perfect day!

"Mary Anne said you went shopping

with someone called Travis," Mum went on. "I'd like you to tell me about it." Mum can be *really* direct when she wants to.

I had to tell them the truth.

"I ran into Travis after school," I said.

"He's a friend of mine, and he asked me if I'd like to drive into town with him—"

"Drive? You went in his car?" Richard interrupted.

"Well, yes. He had to buy a birthday present for his father," I said quickly.

"Who is this Travis?" Mum said. "And how come he can drive?"

"He's old enough to drive," I told her. "He's sixteen."

Wrong move. Richard looked furious, and Mum looked upset.

"Let me get this straight," Richard said slowly. "You went out with a sixteen-year-old in a car? A boy we don't know? You had no business going off like that without asking us first."

I shrugged. This was getting complicated. (And deep down, I had the nagging feeling that Mum was right.)

"Look, why don't we just forget the whole thing and make dinner? I'll help you," I said, reaching for the salad bowl.

"There's no way we're going to forget this," Mum said. "No one's going to eat anything until we get this sorted out."

I knew from the look on her face that she meant business. I was really in for it.

7th CHAPTER

Mary Anne wandered into the kitchen and stopped dead in her tracks when she saw me. She had "uh-oh" written all over her face. She took her time opening a tin of cat food for Tigger, her kitten, and I knew she was listening to every word. If only she hadn't told Mum and Richard that I'd been out with Travis!

"We've got a problem here," Richard said flatly. He motioned for me to sit down at the kitchen table.

"I didn't think you would get this upset," I began, but Richard held his hand up.

"You showed very poor judgment, Dawn," he said sternly.

"I know it looks that way, but—"

"I'm very disappointed in you," Mum said. She sat down opposite me. I felt as if I was being attacked from all sides!

"If you met Travis, you'd really like

him," I protested. I stared at my hands, not knowing where to begin. "He's really a nice boy."

Mum stared at Richard. "I'm sure he is, but that's not the point."

Mary Anne took a quick peek over her shoulder and went back to feeding Tigger. I couldn't believe all the trouble she'd got me into.

"Then what's wrong with him?"

"For one thing, he's too old for you," Richard said bluntly. "He's sixteen and you're only thirteen. What could you possibly have in common?"

"Well, we're both from California. We're interested in the same things." I glanced at Mum, wondering if she would agree with me. She should be able to understand how I felt. Even though I love my friends in Connecticut, I miss my friends in California. So does she.

"And another thing," Mum said, "we've never even met this boy. Did you know he was going to pick you up at school today?"

I shrugged. "Nope. That's just the way Travis is. He likes to do things on the spur of the moment. He's impulsive." *And fun and exciting*, I wanted to add.

"If he really liked you," Richard said, "he would make plans to see you. He'd visit you here at the house and meet the rest of your family."

I sighed. Richard is very serious about

being a good stepfather, but sometimes he just worries too much. I wish he would calm down a little and be more like Mum.

"Travis *does* like me," I said. "You wouldn't believe all the presents he's given me. First a necklace and hair combs, and today he bought me some earrings in town."

"I'm not so sure I like that idea," Mum said slowly. "You hardly know him, and he's showering you with presents. Something just isn't right."

I glanced at Mary Anne, who had finished feeding Tiger and was slipping out of the kitchen. I couldn't *wait* to talk to her alone! None of this would have happened if she had kept her mouth shut.

"It's no mystery," I said, scraping my chair back and standing up. "Travis gave me some presents because he likes me. I don't know why you can't understand that." I looked at Mum. "And I *really* want to see him again."

"I know you do, honey," she said, softening a little. "And I'm sure that once we meet him, we'll feel differently."

"You mean you're going to let her continue to see him?" Richard exploded. "I can't believe you're serious."

"Well, maybe we came down a little hard on him," Mum said hesitantly. She cupped her chin in her hands and looked thoughtful. "You know, he really does sound nice—"

"This is ridiculous!" Richard broke in. "We don't know this boy at all."

"Now, Richard," Mum said soothingly. "Maybe we're making too big a deal out of this. As long as Dawn understands that she can't see him without our permission, I don't think there's any problem."

"Of course there's a problem. She shouldn't be seeing him at all. He's too old for her."

They were still arguing when I quietly slipped out of the kitchen. It was obvious that the argument was going to go on for a long time, and there was someone I wanted to talk to: Mary Anne. I found her upstairs, sprawled on her bed, doing her homework.

"Thanks a lot," I told her. "You really got me into trouble with Mum and Richard."

"Oh, Dawn, you know I didn't want to do that," she said, sitting up. "I feel awful that they're angry with you, but I didn't know what else to say."

"Why did you have to tell them anything?" I asked, slamming my books on her desk. "You could have kept your mouth shut."

"But how could I have?" Mary Anne said in a quavery voice. "They asked me if I knew where you were. So I had to tell them the truth. I said you'd gone shopping. With Travis."

I sighed. I knew Mary Anne couldn't have made up a good lie. Besides, I didn't want her lying for me."

"Anyway, you never said it was a secret." Mary Anne's voice shook a little, and her eyes had grown very bright. "Sharon and Dad would have been really worried about you if I'd told them I didn't know where you were."

"I know," I said wearily. I had a feeling Mary Anne was about to start crying.

"You know I wouldn't do anything to hurt you," she said, sniffling. Mary Anne cries *very* easily. I didn't say anything for a moment, and then I realized that Mary Anne was right. It wasn't her fault that I was in such a mess.

"Look," I said, putting my arm around her shoulders, "why don't we just forget about it? There's really nothing else you could have done."

She looked up, her eyes teary. "Do you mean that?"

I nodded and sat down on her bed. "How was your day? I've hardly seen you."

"Logan came round after school," she said, brightening up a little. "He gave me that toy for Tigger, just like he promised."

Logan is one of the most dependable people I know. He and Mary Anne are a lot alike. You can always count on them, and you always know where you stand with them.

"You really like him, don't you?" I said, even though I knew what her answer would be.

"Of course I do." Mary Anne blushed a little. "I suppose that seems silly to you. He's not exciting, like Travis."

"I don't think it's silly. I like Logan."

"He's not full of surprises," Mary Anne said slowly. "But that's okay with me."

I thought about all the problems Travis had caused me today. "Maybe surprises aren't such a good idea after all," I said.

Mum called us for dinner just then, and we didn't have a chance to talk about Logan and Travis any more. I slid into my place at the dining room table and had no idea what to expect. Would Mum and Richard argue all through dinner? Would I get a lecture? Would they criticize Travis?

Luckily, none of these things happened, and dinner went fairly smoothly, considering the circumstances. But Mum and Richard didn't say much during the meal. Mum just stared at a spot over my head, and Richard pretended to be absorbed in his Greek salad. Mary Anne and I exchanged a look now and then, but neither one of us felt much like talking. However, I had the feeling that this wasn't the last I would hear about Travis.

8th CHAPTER

Saturday

Today I babysat for my younger brothers and sisters and they had a terrific time outdoors playing one of Karen's favourite games -- "Going Camping." It's easy because it's mostly make-believe. All we used today were an old bedspread, some chairs, a few props, and lots of imagination. Karen supplied plenty of that! The best part is that big kids and little kids can play, and it can go on for hours. I think the only other thing you need is a sunny day, but come to think of it, you could probably move the tent into the living room!

Kristy always likes to give a lot of details about her babysitting jobs because she expects the club members to read the notebook very carefully. It's a great way to learn what other babysitters are doing with their kids, and you can get a lot of good ideas. None of us really likes to write in the notebook, but Kristy takes her job as chairman very seriously, and she tries to set an example for us.

"Going Camping" was the perfect way to entertain her four younger brothers and sisters. Karen has a great imagination and loves *any* kind of game that involves "let's pretend." David Michael is an easygoing kid who will go along with just about any game you suggest. And Andrew and Emily love to play, full stop!

This is the way Kristy and Karen set up the game. They found an old bedspread upstairs in the linen cupboard. It had belonged to Andrew and was bright yellow with racing cars all over it.

"It doesn't look like a real tent," David Michael said doubtfully when Kristy and Karen brought it downstairs. "It should be dark green, or maybe brown."

"No, this is fine," Kristy said hastily. She knew the kids were getting restless, and she wanted to start things moving as quickly as possible.

"I'll help!" Karen yelled when Kristy

started to drape the bedspread over some garden chairs.

"Make it a *big* tent," David Michael suggested. "Then we can move all our supplies inside." He picked up a brown canvas canteen and a cast-iron frying pan.

"Big ant?" Emily said, puzzled. Emily is learning English quite slowly. The paediatrician says she's language-delayed.

Andrew laughed. "No, big *tent*," he said, pointing to the bedspread. "C'mon inside."

"Wait! Don't go in yet!" Karen said urgently.

Kristy looked startled. "Why not?"

Karen lowered her voice to a whisper. "Because you can't just walk into a tent without looking. You have to check it first for bears. There could be one sleeping inside."

"Bears?" Emily started to look a little worried.

"It's just pretend," Kristy said, taking her hand. Karen is *very* imaginative, and when you set up a pretend situation, she jumps right in. "What should we do?" Kristy asked very seriously. She was still holding onto Emily's hand. She didn't want to squelch Karen's imagination, but she didn't want Emily to be frightened, either.

Karen thought for a moment. "I'll go in first," she said. She picked up a broken torch. "If I'm not back in a few minutes, you'd better call the mountain rescuers."

"Good idea," David Michael told her. "I think I can signal them. It's a good thing I know Morse code." He scrambled through a cigar box filled with toys and picked out a set of fake teeth. He clicked the teeth together a few times. "We're lucky this is still working."

"I want to do Morse code! I want to do Morse code!" Andrew shouted.

"Sssh," Karen said. "You'll wake up the bear if he's sleeping inside. Do you know how angry they get if you wake them up when they're hibernating? That's all we need!"

"Sorry," Andrew said, clapping his hand over his mouth. "Please can I do Morse code?" he whispered.

David Michael handed him the plastic teeth. "Just remember that SOS is three short, three long, and three short. You got it?" He clicked the teeth together to show him.

"I've got it."

"Places everyone," Karen said. "I'm going in now. Andrew, are you ready?"

"I'm ready with my teeth. I mean the Morse code!"

"David Michael?"

"I'm standing by with the—" He spotted a pile of branches nearby. "The bonfire!"

"Why do we need a bonfire?" Kristy asked.

David Michael rolled his eyes. "In case

the Morse code doesn't work. I can always light the bonfire and use smoke signals to get the mountain ranger."

"Oh, right. Good idea." Kristy smiled to herself. The kids were *really* getting into it. She could hardly wait to tell the BSC members this at the next club meeting.

"Me, too!" Me, too! Me, too!" Emily said, tugging at Karen's T-shirt.

"She wants something to do," Kristy said. "Let's give her a job."

"I know. You can wish me luck. I have a very dangerous job ahead of me," Karen said seriously. She walked over to Emily and shook hands. "Say 'Good luck'," she prompted.

"Good luck," Emily said, smiling. Kristy had no idea if she knew what 'good luck' meant, but she knew Emily was happy to be included.

"Here goes," Karen said dramatically. She took a deep breath and crawled inside the tent. Everyone else crouched down and waited outside, ready to run, if necessary. A few moments passed, and then Karen reappeared. "It's all safe," she said. "There are no bears inside. At least not right this minute."

"What do you mean, right this minute?" David Michael asked.

Karen looked over her shoulders as if she expected a bear to appear at any moment. "I don't want to scare anyone," she said slowly, "but I have to warn you that I found a pot of honey inside."

"Honey!" Andrew clapped his hands over his mouth.

Karen nodded. "And you know what that means," she said, looking round the group.

"What does it mean?" David Michael looked blank.

Karen nudged him. "It means there must have been a *bear* in there."

"Oh, right." David Michael scuffed the dirt with his toe and looked a little embarrassed. "So what do we do now?"

"Well, I think we should all go into the tent," Karen said, holding the flap open. "But make sure you rig up a bear alert outside for us."

"A bear alert?" David Michael brightened. "That's a great idea. You go in and I'll make one."

Kristy trooped inside with the younger kids, and for a minute everyone was quiet. It was pretty hot and uncomfortable in the tent, and she wondered what Karen was going to come up with next. Luckily she didn't have to wait long.

Emily was yawning when Karen grabbed Kristy's arm. "Did you feel that?"

"Feel what?" Kristy asked.

"The ground just shook," Karen said, looking at each of the kids. "I think we're in for an earthquake."

66

"No!" Andrew screamed. "What should we do?"

"Let's all hold hands," Karen said calmly. "That way nobody will be swept away when it happens again."

Emily glanced at Kristy, her eyes wide as saucers, and Kristy scooped her onto her lap. "Don't worry, Emily," she said, holding her very tightly. "I'm not going to let anything happen to you."

"There it goes again," Karen said. She fell against the side of the tent, and Andrew did the same thing. "Hold on tight, everybody!"

"Wait a minute," Andrew yelled. "What about David Michael? He's outside making that stupid bear alert!"

"We'll have to help him," Karen said firmly. "Andrew, rescue David Michael."

Andrew looked impressed. "Wow!"

"Open the flap of the tent *very* carefully and peep outside. The minute you see him, tell him to get in here."

"Okay." Andrew crawled to the edge of the tent and lifted the bedspread. "David Michael! David Michael!" he whispered. "Come inside. I've got to rescue you." He crawled back inside. "He's not there!"

"Are you sure?" Karen asked.

"I'm sure!"

Karen sighed. "This is much worse than I thought."

"Do you think the earthquake got him?" Andrew asked.

"No, I think . . . Morbidda Destiny got him!"

Kristy tried not to laugh. Morbidda Destiny is the old lady who lives next door. Her real name is Mrs Porter, but Karen is convinced that she's a witch. She lives in an old Victorian house with gables and turrets, and she even keeps a broomstick on the front porch.

"Now what will we do?" asked Andrew.

Karen looked stumped. "I don't know. Morbidda Destiny has special powers. She could turn David Michael into a witch if she wanted to, or she might make him drink a magic potion."

"No!"

Karen nodded. "She might even make boy stew out of him."

"Ugh! Gross," Andrew muttered. "How can we save him?"

"Let me think," Karen said, just as the tent flap opened and David Michael crawled in.

"The bear alert is in place," he said, scooting over to Kristy. "You'll all be safe."

"Are you okay?" Karen asked him. "We thought Morbidda Destiny had got you."

David Michael laughed. "Of course I'm okay."

Karen looked at him suspiciously, as if he really might be a newt or a toad pretending to be David Michael. "I suppose so. Where were you when Andrew called you?"

"I was hiding," he said teasingly. "I knew you'd think that Morbidda Destiny had kidnapped me, and I wanted to see what you'd do about it."

"Well, it wasn't funny," Karen said sternly. Andrew started telling David Michael about the earthquake, and Karen sat down next to Kristy. "You know what I think?" she whispered in Kristy's ear. "I think Morbidda Destiny really *did* get him and made him *say* that he was hiding!"

"Do you really think so?" asked Kristy.

Karen nodded. "Witches have their ways," she said mysteriously.

9th
CHAPTER

"You've got to give Chewy a doggie treat or he's going to ruin the play!" Myriah cried.

It was a Thursday afternoon, and I was babysitting for the three younger Hobart kids while Ben was at the dentist. Mathew, James, and Johnny were in the back garden rehearsing their play with Myriah and Gabbie Perkins.

"We can give him a dog biscuit if you want," I suggested, "but I don't think it'll help." Chewbacca, the hero of the play, was tearing around and around the garden. I've never seen a dog with less acting ability. He was supposed to act sad and lonely (according to the script James wrote), but he was running round in circles, yapping and wagging his tail. Every once in a while he'd snap at an imaginary fly.

"Come here, Chewy," I said wearily. "Let's see if this calms you down." I popped a doggie treat into his mouth. He immediately sat up on his hind legs and begged for more.

"I told you it wouldn't help," James said. "That dog can't act."

"He can!" Myriah put her arms around Chewy's furry neck. "He just doesn't feel like it."

"Let's take it from the top. Start the shopping centre scene again," James ordered. "Does everybody remember what they're supposed to do?" He glanced at his notes. "Gabbie, you own a shoe shop."

"Shoes, shoes," she sang. I put my fingers to my lips to remind her to be quiet, and she grinned at me.

"Mathew, you work in the pizza place, and Johnny, you work in a pet shop."

"I want to work in a pet shop!" said Gabbie. "Pets for sale! Pets for sale! We have rabbits, gerbils, and hamsters. Maybe even cats and dogs . . ."

"No, Gabbie," James said quietly. "You stay in your shoe shop and sell shoes. You have a very important part in the play." Gabbie beamed. That was the best thing that James could have said to her.

"Now can we *please* begin?" James said.

"Shoe sale! Shoe sale!" Gabbie chanted. "Come and buy some shoes. We have special offers today."

"Myriah, you can make your entrance now," James said. "Quiet, everybody." He sat down next to me at the picnic table. Nobody moved. "Myriah, what are you waiting for?" he yelled.

She stared at him, her hand on Chewy's neck. "We're waiting for you to cue us," she said. "That's the way they do it in films. You're supposed to say, "And . . . action!""

James rolled his eyes. "All right, all right," he muttered. "And . . . action!"

I smiled.

The scene started smoothly. Myriah was talking softly to Chewy, asking if he was lost, when suddenly earsplitting rock music filled the air.

"Who turned on that radio?" James demanded. He jumped up and raced over to Mathew, who was sitting in a red wagon. "Mathew, what do you think you're doing?" He reached into the wagon and pulled out a small radio. "You're ruining the scene. We can't hear Myriah's lines."

Matthew shrugged. "I'm playing music in my pizza parlour."

Myriah frowned. "Mathew, you can't make any noise when someone else is saying their lines. That's the first thing you have to learn when you put on a play."

"But I don't have anything to do. Nobody gave me any lines."

"You have lines in the next scene," James told him. "Look, all you have to do right now is stay in your place and act as if you're making pizzas."

"I know what I could do," Matthew said. "If you give me my radio back, I could listen to music through my headphones."

James hesitated. "I suppose that would be okay. Just make sure you pay attention so you don't miss your cue. Myriah's going to visit all the shops in the arcade, and you're the second place she goes."

Myriah shifted impatiently. "Can we start again now? Chewy's getting restless."

"Okay," James said. I could tell he was getting annoyed at all the interruptions. "Places everyone."

"You're at it again? I don't believe it!" exclaimed a voice.

I turned to see Zach steering his bike towards the picnic table, where James and I were sitting. "I thought you'd had enough of this baby stuff the other day."

"It's not baby stuff," Myriah said, insulted. "We're putting on a *real* play."

"Yeah, yeah." Zach plopped himself down next to James and punched him playfully in the arm. "So, how about a game of football?"

"He can't leave rehearsal," Myriah said. "We're right in the middle of a very important scene."

"I bet!" Zach snorted. "What kind of a play has a *dog* in it? You must be doing *Annie*."

"No. I've already told you. It's a play I wrote myself," James said shyly. Zach doubled up with laughter and nearly fell off the picnic bench.

"I know, I know." He socked James again, this time on the shoulder. "When are you going to grow up and do some boy stuff?"

"Boy stuff?"

Zach leaned close to him. "You know, football, skateboarding, things like that."

"I play a lot of sports," James said stiffly. I could tell he was embarrassed because two little spots of colour had appeared on his cheeks.

"You could have fooled me!" Zach hooted. "Every time I see you, you're hanging around with a group of girls." He paused. "You know, you're never going to be popular at this rate. The kids at school still think you're weird."

"Weird?"

Zach nodded. "Can you blame them? You don't talk properly, you don't go out with the boys, and worst of all, you hang around with girls."

James hung his head and looked sheepish. "I don't want anybody to think I'm weird."

"Well, of course you don't," Zach said, slapping him on the back. "But you can change all that. Just start doing things differently. And you can start right now."

"I can?"

"Sure." Zach stood up and got on his bike. "Come back to my house and we'll

74

kick a football around. Then we'll watch a new horror film I've just hired. Oh, yeah, and we'll practise talking real American." He released the kickstand on his bike, ready to go. "Sound good?"

James hesitated, and then tossed his script on the picnic table. "You're on!" he said.

"James," Myriah wailed. "What about the play?"

James shook his head and didn't answer. He was already on the way to the garage for his bike.

"Now what will we do?" Mathew asked. "We can't put on the play without James."

"We'll think of something else to do," I promised him. I watched as Zach and James pedalled down the drive. Why did James let Zach talk to him like that? And why did he want to change his whole personality to please Zach? James was a great kid, just the way he was. Zach had no business telling him how to talk or how to act. Why did James let him get away with it? None of it made any sense to me, and I was *very* disappointed in James.

Kristy had dropped a bombshell and didn't even know it. It all started at our Monday afternoon BSC meeting in Claudia's room. Jessi mentioned Jackie Rodowsky, the "walking disaster", and everyone started telling funny stories about him. In case you don't know, Jackie is a really sweet seven-year-old with flaming red hair and freckles. He's also accident-prone.

"Do you remember the day I took Jackie to the pool?" Kristy said. "First he got stung by a bee, and then he got lost and almost gave me a heart attack. My brother Sam told one of the girls in his class about it, and she said she saw the whole thing. She was working as a lifeguard that day."

"Really? Who was it?" Mary Anne asked.

"I don't know her name, but she's this *fantastic*-looking girl who's captain of the swimming team at Stoneybrook High

School." Kristy picked up her clipboard, ready to get back to business. "Sam says she's the reason Travis tried out for swimming along with all his other sports. I hear he's really crazy about her. They've been going out together for weeks."

I looked up from the club notebook in total shock. Travis was going out with someone? Travis was *crazy* about someone? How could that be possible? He was interested in *me*! I could feel my cheeks burning, and I wondered if anyone else had noticed. I started thumbing through a *Seventeen* magazine, hoping Kristy wouldn't get annoyed with me.

The club meeting went on as usual and a few minutes later, I actually managed to take a phone call from Dr Johanssen, who needed a sitter for Charlotte. My voice sounded a little shaky, but I wrote down all the details about the job and promised to call her back.

"Now, who gets the job?" Kristy asked brightly, as Mary Anne checked the record book.

I returned to the *Seventeen* magazine, dying for the meeting to be over. What was going on with Travis? Could Kristy be mistaken? I couldn't wait to get home and work everything out in my head.

Unfortunately, Mum asked me to make a salad the minute I walked through the door. It was the last thing in the world I felt like doing, but what could I say? Mary Anne made spaghetti, Mum made the sauce (meatless), Richard made garlic bread, and before I knew it, all four of us were eating dinner together.

I was there, but I wasn't there. Does that make sense? I was sitting at the dining room table, passing the salad and half listening to Mary Anne talk about school, but my mind was a million miles away. I could have been on another planet! My brain was churning, trying to come up with an explanation for what Kristy had said about Travis.

I hated to admit it, but there just weren't that many possibilities. I didn't really think that Kristy had made a mistake, because she had seemed so definite about it. She had mentioned Travis by name (and how many Travises could there be at SHS?).

Then I let my mind play a little game. Maybe there was a weird reason for Travis's behaviour. Maybe he was just pretending to like this girl. But why? I was stumped. Unless . . . maybe Travis *wanted* to join the swimming team, too, and he thought one way to do it would be to go out with the captain. But wait a minute. Travis was a great athlete (he said so himself), so why would he need to do that? Nothing made sense. There *was* no explanation for the way Travis was acting.

I said so later that evening to Mary Anne, when we were upstairs working hard in my room. (Sometimes we do our homework together.) That night, Mary Anne was solving maths problems, and I was thinking about Travis.

"You know, it just doesn't make sense," I blurted out.

"What doesn't?" Mary Anne hardly looked up from her book.

"What Kristy said about Travis and that lifeguard!" My voice was so loud it startled her.

"Oh, that." She pushed her papers aside and stared at me.

"Well, what did you think about it?" I said impatiently.

Mary Anne shrugged. "I suppose I didn't think much about it either way. Did it bother you?"

Did it bother me! "Yes," I said with clenched teeth. "It bothered me a lot."

Mary Anne sighed. "Then I wish she hadn't brought it up."

"No, I'm glad she did. Maybe this way I can work out what's going on. I don't know why he's taking someone else out. And I'm not sure why he's been paying so much attention to me." I was pacing restlessly back and forth in front of the dressing table.

"Dawn, it's not the end of the world. I wish you weren't so unhappy about it." Sometimes Mary Anne gets really upset over other people's problems, but she's usually a good person to talk to.

"But I thought Travis cared about *me*!"

Mary Anne hesitated. "I'm sure he does. But he can take out anyone he wants to. It's not as if the two of you are going steady. Anyway, she's probably a lot closer to him in age."

"But why is he paying so much attention to me? I thought he really liked me."

"I suppose he likes her, too. There's nothing wrong with that, is there?"

I was all ready to argue, and then I stopped myself. What Mary Anne was saying made sense, even though it hurt to admit it. Travis and I didn't have a formal relationship the way Mary Anne and Logan have. In a way, I envy Mary Anne, because she always knows where she stands with Logan. And he knows where he stands with her. But Travis is the kind of boy who keeps you guessing. He's full of surprises (the lifeguard was a big one!), and I'd have to find a way to handle it.

Later that night, as I turned out my light, the idea came to me in a flash. The best way to find out how Travis felt about this girl was to see the two of them together. And that was exactly what I was going to do.

I got my chance a few days later. It was a sunny Thursday afternoon, and my teacher decided to let our class out ten minutes early. I raced across the school yard. If I hurried, I could just get to SHS before the dismissal bell rang.

The SHS kids were rushing down the broad stone steps of the school as I came tearing round the corner. My heart sank. How would I ever find Travis in this huge mob? I was just trying to decide where to stand to get the best view, when I had an incredible stroke of luck. I spotted Travis pausing in the doorway to put on his sunglasses. He looked terrific in faded jeans and a white T-shirt, and my heart did a little flip-flop. I was dying to run up to him and tell him how glad I was to see him.

But he wasn't alone. He turned round and linked arms with a great-looking girl. Her long red hair tumbled down her back, and she had high cheekbones, just like a model. She was dressed in a white cotton flight suit, exactly the kind of trendy outfit that Claudia or Stacey would wear. I hated her on sight. Then I stopped and reminded myself that it wasn't her fault she was gorgeous, or that Travis liked her.

Travis and the girl headed for the pavement and I held my breath, hoping that Travis didn't have his car. Another stroke of luck. They walked right past the school car park, still arm in arm. They were probably going into town (another shopping trip?) and if I was very careful, I'd be able to follow them. I waited behind a tree until they were a good distance ahead of me.

I had to know what Travis was up to.

11th CHAPTER

A few minutes later, I decided I wasn't cut out to be a spy. Do you know how hard it is to follow someone? (I know what you're probably thinking. How can I say that when it looks so easy on television?)

But I had two disasters almost immediately. First, I stepped into a huge puddle, ruining my new shoes, and then I was nearly run over by a dustcart. I was so busy watching Travis that I didn't even notice the lights had changed, and I stepped straight out into the road. How stupid!

I took a deep breath and told myself to calm down. I would never find out the truth about Travis if I were flattened by a lorry. The trick was to stay cool.

I made sure Travis and the girl stayed at least a hundred yards ahead of me. With any luck, I'd be able to blend into the crowd once we got into town. The tricky part was a long stretch of a street with a narrow pavement and very few trees. I knew that if Travis turned round for any reason, he would spot me.

I was being extra cautious when a car horn blasted right behind me. I nearly jumped out of my skin! To my horror, Travis heard it, too. He glanced over his shoulder, and I hardly had time to dart behind a bush. Had he seen me? I had no idea, but I wasn't taking any chances. I crouched behind the bush, feeling a little silly, but afraid to get up. I counted silently to ten and then took up the chase once more.

A few minutes later we reached Stoneybrook town centre. Travis and the girl stopped first at Burger Bite, and I watched them go into a back booth. Would he order for her? I wondered. I took a seat near the front door and peered out from underneath a giant menu. If I scrunched around in my seat, I could see them in the mirror.

They were laughing and talking, and when the girl picked up the menu, Travis put his hand over hers. He winked at her before he gave their order to the waitress. My heart sank. The smiles, the tender looks . . . it was all so familiar. Travis was staring at her as if she were the only girl in the room. He had looked at me in exactly the same way!

I gulped down a lemonade and quietly left the restaurant. My heart was pounding in my chest as I sat on a bench across the street from the Burger Bite. I decided to wait for them to come out and then follow them to their next stop. Why was I doing this? I can't explain it. I just *had* to know what they were going to do next, even though I knew it was going to hurt me.

About half an hour later, they came out arm in arm and headed for the Jewellery Shop. Hamburgers and pierced earrings. Sounds familiar, doesn't it? Travis was taking her to *exactly* the same places he had taken me. I wondered for one crazy moment if Travis would even buy her the same earrings he had bought for me. (Not that it would matter at this point.)

They didn't buy anything, but they wandered up and down the aisles, looking at the jewellery. They kept their heads close together, laughing and talking. Even though I couldn't hear what they were saying, I could see that they were having a terrific time together. Why couldn't I have been the one with Travis? My chest felt so tight, I thought it would explode, but I forced myself to keep watching them. I should have known that things could only get worse.

It was late afternoon when they finally finished their window shopping and headed away from town. I tagged along after them, feeling tired and discouraged. (And very jealous.) There were so many thoughts crowding in my head at once that it was impossible to think clearly. Why was Travis so interested in this girl? Yes, I know she was great-looking, but it had to be more than that. Travis had told me again and again how beautiful my eyes were, and he had even picked out combs for me to wear in my hair. So that must mean that he thought I was pretty good-looking, didn't it? What did she have that I didn't have?

I was trying to sort everything out when Travis and the girl suddenly entered a small park. I barely had time to duck into a bus shelter when the two of them sat down on a bench just a few feet away. Now what?

I didn't have to wait long. I watched in horror as Travis leaned over and *kissed* her! I know I gasped out loud, but both of them were too busy to notice. My hand flew up to my mouth, and I felt hot tears stinging my eyelids. How could this be happening?

I don't know how long they would have stayed in the park, but suddenly a group of little kids sat down next to them. I saw Travis frown and then laughingly pull the redhead to her feet. She laid her head against his shoulder, just for a moment, and then the two of them moved off again, arm in arm. I felt like staying there in the bus shelter and crying my eyes out, but I knew I had to keep going.

After a few yards, they stopped at the cinema and looked at the marquee. The way they were nodding and talking, it was obvious that they were making plans to see a film together. That night? That weekend? I had no way of knowing, but it didn't really matter. All that mattered was that *she* would be with Travis, and I wouldn't. Their fingers were laced tightly together, and I saw the look in Travis's eyes when he smiled at her. He should be smiling that way at *me*.

I had seen enough. It was nearly dusk, and I hurried home, thinking, thinking, thinking. Did Travis like this girl because she was his own age? Was I really "too young" for him, just like Richard had said? Was Travis annoyed with me because I hadn't taken his advice and had that third hole pierced in my ear? Surely he wouldn't get so annoyed over a little thing like that? No matter how hard I tried to explain things, my mind kept coming back to one point: Travis didn't care about me at all. How could I have been so wrong about him?

I was still *very* upset over Travis when we had our next BSC meeting. I had made up my mind not to say anything to my friends, but somehow everything came pouring out.

We were waiting around for phone calls when Kristy mentioned that Sam and Travis were on the track team together. "I don't know how Travis does it," Kristy said admiringly. "He's playing three different sports this season, and he's even talking about auditioning for the school play."

"He should," Stacey piped up. "Can you imagine how great he'd look on stage? He's gorgeous! He's got the dreamiest eyes I've ever seen."

Stacey (who happens to be a little boy-crazy) was all set to launch into a long description of Travis's smile, when I cut her off.

"Please, can we change the subject?" I pleaded. I jumped up and grabbed my jacket. "If we're just going to sit around and talk about boys, I'm going home. I've got better things to do."

Kristy looked shocked, and Stacey gave me a long look. "Dawn, what's wrong?" she asked.

"Nothing," I snapped. I turned round so that my friends couldn't see the tears that were threatening to spill down my cheeks. "I've just heard enough about Travis, that's all. In fact, I've heard *more* than enough!" I stumbled blindly towards the door to Claudia's room, but Mary Anne stopped me.

"Wait, Dawn," she said softly. "You might as well tell everyone what's going on."

"I don't want to talk about it," I said stiffly.

Mary Anne took my hand and pulled me gently on to Claud's bed. "That's what friends are for, you know. We're all here for each other."

I hesitated. Everyone was looking at me, and they all seemed worried. Maybe it *was* better to get things out into the open.

"I saw Travis with someone else," I said slowly. "Probably the captain of the swimming team. That's why I'm so upset."

Stacey looked puzzled. "Why would that bother you? Unless—" She clapped her hand over her mouth. "Are you going out with him? Oh, wow! When did all this happen?"

I shrugged. "We're not really going out together, but I know he cares about me. I mean, I *thought* he cared about me." I told them about the surprise visit at the house, and the necklace and hair combs. (Also the trip to Burger Bite and the Jewellery Shop.) I left out the part about Mum and Richard being so angry with me.

"That rat," Stacey said angrily after I told them about Travis kissing the girl in the park. "Why did he lead you on like that?"

"He didn't really lead her on," Kristy said. "Don't forget, he never really asked her out. At least, not on a real date."

"Oh, Kristy," Claudia said. "You're being much too practical. If somebody visits you at your house and brings you presents, it's like a date. And if they take you shopping after school, that's like a date, too."

88

"It is?" Jessi asked. She and Mallory had been following the whole conversation without saying a word.

Claudia unwrapped a Murray Mint and popped it into her mouth. "Well, sort of. At least I think it is."

"I think so, too," Stacey said. "Travis gave Dawn the idea that he liked her, so he's definitely a creep."

I sighed. I was glad that my friends were all taking my side, but I didn't feel much better. My chest ached every time I thought about Travis.

"Don't worry, Dawn," Claudia said. "You'll meet someone a million times nicer than Travis. Someone who *appreciates* you."

I sniffled a little. How could there be anybody nicer than Travis?

"In fact," Mary Anne said, "I think I know just the person."

"You do?" Kristy asked. "Tell us about him."

Mary Anne grinned. "Well, he's fourteen, and he's fantastic-looking. And he's got a great sense of humour, and he's supposed to be *really* nice."

"Supposed to be?" Kristy raised her eyebrows. "Don't you know for sure?

"I'm sure" said Mary Anne. "It's just that I haven't met him yet."

"Who is he?" Jessi asked. "Does he go to SMS?"

"No, he lives outside town." She paused. "He's Logan's cousin. His name is Lewis and he's coming here for a visit soon." She bent down so we were on eye level. "And guess what? He hasn't got a girlfriend."

Mary Anne looked quite pleased with herself. I didn't want to sound ungrateful, but I had no desire to meet Lewis. I didn't care how nice he was or how handsome or funny. I wanted Travis. Why couldn't everyone understand that?

"Isn't it wonderful?" Mary Anne went on, all smiles.

I blew my nose and tried to look interested. There was no point in hurting Mary Anne's feelings, and I could always make up some excuse for not seeing Lewis when he got here.

"Wonderful," I said. "Just wonderful."

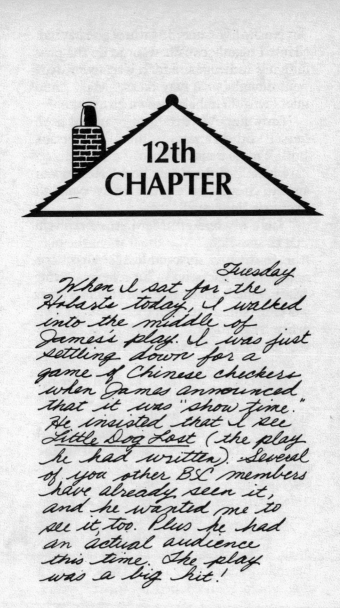

12th CHAPTER

Tuesday

When I sat for the Hobarts today, I walked into the middle of James's play. I was just settling down for a game of Chinese checkers when James announced that it was "show time." He insisted that I see <u>Little Dog Lost</u> (the play he had written). Several of you other BSC members have already seen it, and he wanted me to see it, too. Plus he had an actual audience this time. The play was a big hit!

"Please, Mary Anne," Mathew and Myriah chanted together. "We want to do the play for a big audience today. It's really ready."

"I thought we'd play chess," Mary Anne said, "and then make brownies together."

"Brownies! We can have brownies *anytime*," said Myriah. "This is important stuff. This is a play!"

"Please!" Gabbie squealed. "No brownies! No chess! Don't you want everyone to see *Little Dog Lost*?"

"Well, of course," Mary Anne replied. "Of course I do." She knew about the play from reading Kristy's and Jessi's babysitting notes. They had seen it "in rehearsal" and Mary Anne realized that the kids had been working on it a lot since then.

She glanced at James, who was looking very pleased with himself. "Are you ready to do this?"

He nodded. "As ready as we'll ever be. Everybody knows their lines, and if Chewy stays under control, we'll be fine."

Chewy! Mary Anne's heart sank. She had forgotten that Chewy was the star of the play. "Where is Chewy?" Mary Anne asked.

"He's all ready!" Gabbie informed her. "He's waiting in the garage." She looked at James. "We call that offstage."

"I see." Mary Anne watched as Gabbie opened the garage door and Chewy came barrelling across the garden. He acted like a dog who'd been cooped up for five years.

He immediately began running round in circles.

"He's excited," Myriah explained.

"I can see that." Mary Anne gently pushed Chewy off the garden chair he'd jumped on. "Are you sure he'll calm down enough for the play?"

"I know he will," Myriah said, petting him. "I'll put him back in the garage."

Mary Anne doubted that Chewy would calm down but she didn't want to discourage Myriah. "Okay," she said finally, "where do we start?"

"We need to set up chairs for the audience, and then we need to start ringing doorbells." James was suddenly very businesslike as he dragged some folding chairs over to the patio. "This is the stage," he said, motioning to the back garden, "and this is where the audience sits."

"That looks fine, but what did you mean about ringing doorbells?"

"To tell people about the play," said Mathew impatiently.

"We should really have sent out invitations," Myriah said, "but we've been so busy rehearsing, we didn't get round to it." She looked a little worried. "It's not too late to ask people to come, is it?"

"I suppose not." Mary Anne glanced at her watch. It was after three-thirty. "But we'd better get started straight away. How about if I phone Mallory Pike to see if she can bring some of her brothers and sisters?"

"Oh, good!" Myriah clapped her hands together. "And ask Jessi to bring Becca and Squirt."

"The more the better," James said. "The grown-ups can sit on the folding chairs, and the little kids can sit on blankets."

"Are we inviting grown-ups?" asked Mary Anne.

"Of course! Otherwise it won't seem like a real play," James replied.

"Hmm, I suppose you're right." Where could Mary Anne find some real live parents at a moment's notice? she wondered. She thought of Mrs Pike. As far as she knew, Mal's mum was the only one of our clients who might be at home.

A quick phone call to Mrs Pike settled things.

"Of course I'll come, Mary Anne," she said warmly. "Stacey took a couple of kids to the playground, but I'll round them up along with Vanessa and the triplets. I know they'd love to see a play."

Half an hour later, everything was falling into place. Mal (who was babysitting for Charlotte Johannsen) arrived with Charlotte and her best friend, Becca Ramsey. Jessi brought the Newton kids. Stacey arrived a few minutes later with two of the Pike kids—Margo, who's seven, and Claire, who's five.

"Hi, Mary Anne-silly-billy-goo-goo!"

Claire shouted. (Claire is going through an extremely silly stage at the moment.)

Mary Anne was helping everyone find seats when Claudia appeared. "I've just heard about the play," Claud whispered. "I'll help seat people if you want to go and help James. He looks as if he's got a problem."

Mary Anne glanced up. James was darting back and forth with a clipboard, barking orders to his actors. "Johnny, I want you to be quiet until it's time for you to say your lines!"

"*Little dog lost*," he sang softly.

James put his finger to his lips. "No talking," he said sternly.

"I wasn't talking. I was singing," Johnny said, making a face.

James looked as if he wanted to throw his clipboard in the air. Mary Anne touched his shoulder. "I'll make sure the younger kids are in their places," she told him. "Why don't you do something about Chewy? He's making a racket in the garage, and I'm afraid someone's going to let him out."

"Let him out?" Myriah repeated. "Oh, no!" She grabbed a Magic Marker and a piece of paper and told Mary Anne to make a sign that read: STAR'S DRESSING ROOM. KEEP OUT!

Mary Anne smiled. "I think that'll do it," she said.

The audience was settling down and James edged over to Mary Anne.

"Do you think I should say something to the audience?" He looked a little nervous.

Mary Anne nodded. "You'll have to introduce the play. After all, they don't even have programmes."

"I feel a little silly."

"Don't feel silly. And remember to tell everyone that you *wrote* the play."

"Do you think so?"

"Of course. You should be very proud. Not many kids your age could write a play."

James smiled then, and Mary Anne knew he was relaxing a little. A few minutes later, he cleared his throat and stepped in front of the crowd. Mary Anne crossed her fingers as he finished the introduction and took a seat in the front row. It was show time!

Myriah made her entrance like a professional actress. She was wearing one of Mrs Perkins's coats and carrying a large handbag.

"Oh, I just love shopping in the arcade," she said brightly.

"Hi, Myriah-silly-billy-goo-goo!" Claire shouted from the audience.

Myriah frowned but stayed in character. "Where shall I go first?" she said, coming close to the audience. "There are so many shops to choose from."

Mary Anne knew that Chewy was supposed to be on stage by that point, but there was no sign of him. James turned round from the front row and caught her eye. "Get Chewy fast!" he mouthed.

Mary Anne grabbed Johnny Hobart, who didn't have to go on stage for a while. "Quick, Johnny," Mary Anne hissed. "Let Chewy out of the garage."

Johnny stared at her. "I already have," he said solemnly.

"Then where is he?"

Johnny pointed toward the Perkinses' garden, where Chewy was digging an enormous hole in the flower garden.

"Oh, no!" Mary Anne wailed.

"I can whistle for him," Johnny suggested.

"Do it!"

Johnny stuck two fingers in his mouth and made an earsplitting sound. Chewy bounded across the lawn, knocked over Gabbie's "shoe shop", and skidded to a halt at Johnny's feet.

The kids in the audience started laughing, not sure if this was supposed to be part of the show. Mary Anne knew she had to act fast. She grabbed Chewy's collar and pushed him "on stage".

"Go on. Act as though you're lost," she pleaded.

Myriah waited until Chewy raced over to her, and then she sank down to her knees. "Oh, you poor dog," she cried. "You're lost and looking for your owner." Chewy immediately began licking her face, nearly beside himself with joy. "You must be very . . . sad," she said doubtfully.

Someone in the audience giggled at this line, because Chewy was running in circles and barking. He didn't look in the least bit sad!

Myriah decided to adlib some lines. "Sometimes dogs *act* happy, but they're really sad. And *lost*," she added, in case the little kids in the audience had missed the point.

James signalled to Myriah to begin her walk through the "arcade", and she headed for Gabbie, who was rearranging her shoe shop.

"Shoe sale! Shoe sale!" Gabbie yelled, picking up a decrepit shoe. It was muddy from Chewy's mad dash through the garden. Everybody laughed at her line, and Gabbie looked pleased.

James rolled his eyes. Mary Anne knew the play wasn't turning out at all as he expected, but at least he was getting a lot of laughs. And then *Mary Anne* got a surprise. She was standing at the back of the patio when Zach appeared! He was the last person in the world she wanted to see at the play.

Mary Anne wasn't taking any chances. She showed him to a seat right at the back of the audience, and decided to sit next to him. "It's a great play," she whispered. "Really funny."

"Uh-huh." Zach looked totally unimpressed. He crossed his arms in front of his chest and didn't smile for the next fifteen minutes. Mary Anne couldn't imagine why he had bothered to show up.

The moment the play was over (to wild applause) Zach grabbed James by the arm. "Hey, how about some football?" he said.

"I don't know. I'm a bit busy at the moment," James began.

"C'mon. Drop this baby stuff and let's kick a ball around," said Zach, and James looked completely confused.

Zach pulled James down the drive. Mary Anne didn't know why James let himself be dragged along, or why he didn't speak up. A lot of kids wanted to talk to him about the play, and James was letting Zach ruin his big moment for him. It didn't make sense.

Then Mary Anne thought about Dawn and Travis and got an idea. Dawn would be sure to read the notebook. Maybe this was Mary Anne's chance to tell her some things she'd been thinking about.

Tuesday (con't)
Even though the play
went well, I can't
stop thinking about
James and the way

he let himself be controlled by Zach. I hate to say it, Dawn, but it made me think of you and Travis. Zach is trying to make James into something Zach wants him to be, and, well, can you see that Travis is doing the same thing with you? You know I'm not saying this to hurt your feelings, but it's something you should really think about. Travis is trying to make you into someone you don't want to be. You're great, just the way you are. Please don't let him change you, and don't hang around any more waiting for him to drop by. That's not your style. Kristy, I hope you're not angry

with me for writing
this in the club note-
book, and Dawn, I
hope you're not angry,
either. But it's easier
for me to write this
than to say it. I hope
you understand. And
I hope you'll see Lewis
when he comes to town.

You're probably wondering why I would even *want* to see Travis again after that scene in the park. After all, I'd seen him kissing another girl, so what could be left between us? I was tempted to forget the whole thing (and Travis, too) but I couldn't. I wanted Travis to know that I was on to him, and there was only one way I could do that. I'd have to wait until he left school with the girl and follow them again. But this time would be different. This time, I would confront Travis!

What did I hope to accomplish? Well, if nothing else, I would *embarrass* him! I could just imagine how Travis would react when I bumped into him with his girlfriend. Let's see how cool and confident he'd be then!

I got my chance the following Tuesday afternoon. We had a quiz at the end of the day, and our teacher said we could leave as soon as we handed in our papers. What a lucky break! I whizzed through the test, double-checked my answers (it was a multiplechoice test), and left school fifteen minutes early. I had plenty of time to catch Travis as he left SHS.

My heart was pounding as I waited on a bench near the front steps of the school. I was wearing sunglasses, and I kept my head ducked down. I wanted to make sure that I spotted Travis before he recognized me!

Soon the bell rang, and kids came pouring out of the double doors. I saw Travis and caught my breath. He was alone! My mind raced with possibilities. Maybe he'd broken up with the girl. Maybe he'd realized *I* was the girl he'd wanted all along. Maybe the two of us could spend a wonderful after-noon together. Maybe, maybe, maybe . . .

There I was, lost in fantasyland when Sara (Kristy had found out her name for me) appeared on the scene. She darted up to Travis, and he grabbed her in a big bear hug. They hurried down the steps, just inches away from me. (I didn't need the sunglasses after all, because they never even looked at me. They were too wrapped up in each other.) My heart sank, but I was more determined than ever. It was time to catch Travis out.

I decided that the best place to "bump into" them would be in town. That way I could pretend that I was out shopping. (I certainly didn't want Travis to know that I'd waited for him outside his school.)

Travis and Sara walked briskly along, and I kept a hundred metres or so behind them. I didn't feel nervous at all because I was absolutely sure I was doing the right thing. The only question now was, *where* should I run into them?

I got my chance outside the Jewellery Shop. It was a bright, sunny day, and the shop was holding a sale. Customers were jamming the area in front of the shop, looking for bargains, and Travis and Sara had stopped in front of a display rack.

Travis was pointing to a pair of gold hoop earrings, when I positioned myself on the opposite side of the rack. If I waited a few more seconds, he'd be bound to see me. The moment he gave the rack a little spin, we'd be staring right into each other's eyes!

"I really like the silver hoops better," Sara was saying. I remember thinking what a wispy little-girl voice she had, and then it happened. The rack shifted and Travis and I were face-to-face. The moment of truth at last!

I gave him a casual smile, and to my amazement, he *grinned* back at me. "Hi, Dawn," he said in a friendly way. He didn't sound in the least bit embarrassed! I was baffled, but I tried to be cool.

"Hi, Travis. I suppose this is one of your favourite spots." I thought he deserved a little dig. After all, he'd taken *me* to the Jewellery Shop not too long ago, and now he was back in the same spot (with another girl).

He laughed, totally missing the point. "It does look that way, doesn't it?" Sara, who had been paying no attention to the conversation, suddenly held up a pair of heavy gold hoop earrings.

"What do you think, Travis?" she asked, ignoring me. "Are these too big?"

I couldn't resist. "Yes, definitely too big. They look like they should be holding up a shower curtain."

Sara frowned and gave Travis a "who-is-this-person?" look, and he introduced us.

"Dawn is from California, too," he added.

"Really?" Sara gave me a cool smile. "Oh, now I remember," she said, as if a light bulb had switched on inside her head. "Dawn Schafer . . . the little girl you told me about."

Little girl? I was steaming. What a nerve. I tried to think of a really stinging comeback, but my mind was a blank. And the next words out of Sara's mouth were even worse. I'm sure you've turned her into a real beauty, Travis," she murmured.

That did it! "I was already a beauty," I said hotly. I suppose it was a very conceited thing to say, but I didn't care.

Sara and Travis exchanged an amused

105

look. I have *never* been so embarrassed in my life, and I knew I was making a fool of myself. The only thing to do was get out of there—fast.

"I've got to get home," I muttered.

"Nice to have met you," Sara said. She looked like she was going to burst out laughing the minute my back was turned.

"See you around." Travis grinned at me as if nothing had changed. How could he be so casual when my whole world had turned upside down?

I practically ran all the way home. I felt hurt, angry, upset, and *very* foolish. I didn't say a word during dinner and bounded upstairs to my room the minute the dishes were done.

"You're pretty quiet," Mary Anne said. She had come into my room so softly, I hadn't heard her. I was sprawled on my bed, maths book in hand, but my mind was on Travis and Sara.

"I'm thinking," I told her. I looked at her and then looked away.

She sat down at my desk, watching me. "Did you ever see *My Fair Lady*?" she asked. "You know, the film based on the play *Pygmalion*?"

What was she getting at? I sat up in bed, scrunching a pillow behind my head. "I saw it a long time ago. We got it out on video once."

Mary Anne looked pleased. "Then I

suppose you remember the story. You know how proper Professor Higgins turns Eliza Doolittle, the Cockney girl, into his 'fair lady'?"

"Of course. He changed everything about her, the way she walked and talked and even the way she dressed. He wanted to make her into a real lady."

Mary Anne stared at me. "Well," she said slowly, "I never liked that."

I nodded. "Me neither. Eliza should have been allowed to be herself."

"Exactly."

We were both very quiet, and then it hit me. "I get it," I said. "You're talking about Travis and me." Mary Anne didn't answer, and I thought about it a little more. "He wanted to change me and make me into someone else." I hesitated. "But why did he choose *me*? There were dozens of girls he could have picked."

"Who knows? I think he really liked you at first. Or maybe he was interested because you were from California."

I sighed. Everything was falling into place. Travis had never liked me as much as I had liked him. I was simply a "project" for him. I felt a *little* better, having worked out what was going on, but now I had another problem. What should I do next?

Mary Anne must have read my mind. "I think you should confront him," she said. "Tell him exactly what you think."

"I think so, too. It won't be easy. That's what I thought I was going to do today. But I know it's the right thing to do." I smiled at her. "You've been a big help, Mary Anne."

"I'm glad." She hugged me and headed towards the door. "Oh, and Dawn, there's one more thing you need to do."

"What's that?"

She grinned. "Be sure you read the club notebook."

14th CHAPTER

Now that I'd made up my mind about what to do, I didn't think twice. I didn't make elaborate plans to follow Travis, or think about what I was going to say to him. I just reached for the phone, hoping that the right words would come to me. (Sometimes when you have to say something really hard, it's better not to plan too much.)

"Dawn, how are you?" exclaimed Travis when he picked up the phone.

He acted as if nothing was wrong! His voice was so warm and friendly, I almost lost my cool, but I knew I had to be strong.

"I'm fine," I told him. "In fact, I've always been fine, but it took me a while to realize that."

"Huh?"

I took a deep breath. "You don't get it, do you?" I rushed on. "Well, maybe I can explain it to you."

"Okay, shoot." A tiny note of doubt crept into his voice.

I braced myself for the toughest part of all. "You really hurt me, Travis."

"I *hurt* you?" He sounded incredulous.

"Yes, you did. You told me how to dress, how to do my hair, how to act. You tried to make me into something I'm not."

There was a long pause. "You're right. I don't get it," he said finally. "How could something like that hurt you? You're a great-looking girl, Dawn. I just thought you could use a few suggestions on how to dress and do your hair."

"It was more than a few, but anyway, that's not the point. You can't imagine what a big effect you had on me. I took everything you said to heart." I hesitated, twisting the phone cord around my fingers. "Maybe you can't understand this, Travis, but I practically ran round in circles trying to please you. I tried so hard to be everything you wanted me to be." It's funny, but even as I said the words, I realized that the harder I tried, the more hopeless things had become. I knew now that I could *never* be what Travis wanted (and that I didn't want to be).

Travis gave a little laugh. "Dawn, I really think you're making too much of this. You know, if we could just get together and talk this over, I think you'd see things my way."

"I don't think so," I said quietly.

"You mean you don't want to see me just

because I told you to wear combs in your hair? I can't believe it."

"It's a lot more than that, Travis. Look, I'll give you the perfect example. Remember when you wanted me to get that third hole pierced in my ear? I actually felt guilty because I didn't want to go along with it. I'm just glad I had the brains not to listen to you."

"Dawn, you're making a big deal out of nothing," Travis spluttered. Now he was beginning to sound *really* uncomfortable.

"No, it's true. You've been trying to change me ever since the day you met me," I said, cutting him off. "You wanted to change everything about me. I just didn't see it in the beginning."

"Dawn, this is crazy."

"It's not crazy at all," I said smoothly. "I've had time to think about it, and I've talked things over with Mary Anne. You never liked me for myself, just for what you could make me into. It all makes sense now."

"Look, I never wanted to hurt you, Dawn—"

"Maybe not, but that's what happened. Besides everything else, you led me on. You let me think I was special to you, but you were seeing Sara at the same time." I felt very calm. "Anyway, I think we should just say goodbye now."

"Say goodbye? Are you serious?"

111

"Very serious," I said softly. "That's why I phoned you tonight, Travis. To say goodbye, and to say that I hope you find the perfect girl for you. She's probably out there somewhere, Travis, but I'm not her. Maybe it's Sara."

Travis started to say something, but I didn't give him a chance. I hung up the receiver very gently and stared out of the window for a few minutes.

It was over. And I knew I'd done the right thing.

The reaction at the next BSC meeting was just what I had hoped for.

"Dawn! I can't believe you did it. I'm so proud of you!" Claudia was beaming. "He really got what was coming to him."

"Travis must have been furious," Stacey chimed in. "I wish I could have been there."

"I'm just happy you're rid of him," Mary Anne said. "You finally realized."

"It took a little help from my friends," I added. "For a while, I thought there was something wrong with *me*."

"Ha! That's probably what he wanted you to think," Kristy said. She tilted her visor back. "I had no idea Travis was such a jerk. He hangs around with my brothers all the time."

Mary Anne looked up from the notebook. "Well, he's probably okay when he's with boys because he's not trying to change them."

Kristy nodded. "I suppose you're right. The main thing is that he's out of Dawn's life for good—" I started to giggle, and Kristy stopped in mid-sentence. "What's so funny?"

"I just thought of something I should have said. I should have told Travis to get his hair trimmed and to get rid of those stone-washed jeans. He could do with a few fashion tips himself!"

"You would have been wasting your breath," Stacey said, examining her nail varnish. "He's so conceited, he probably thinks he's perfect."

I was struggling with a maths problem later that night when Mary Anne came into my room. She looked a little embarrassed, and I wondered why.

"How's it going?" She glanced at my maths book, but I knew she had something else on her mind.

"Okay." I closed the book and spun round in my seat. "I can have a break if you want to talk."

"Well . . . yes," Mary Anne said, settling herself on the bed. I waited while she fumbled in her pocket for a white envelope. "I . . . just wanted to tell you again that I'm really proud of the way you handled Travis."

113

I smiled at her. "I'm glad. But I bet that isn't why you came in here."

Mary Anne flushed. "Well, I—Okay, I'll be honest with you. I've got something for you." She glanced at the envelope but drew back when I reached for it. "No, wait! Before you read it, I want to explain something."

From the look on Mary Anne's face, I knew it must be something important. And I knew there was no way I could rush Mary Anne. She would tell me in her own good time.

"Do you remember when I told you about Lewis?"

"Lewis?" I drew a blank, and then it hit me. "Oh, yeah. Logan's cousin. What about him?"

"Well, guess what? His visit to Stoneybrook is all planned!"

"Really?" I know Mary Anne expected me to look thrilled, but I just couldn't. My hand edged back to the maths book. I had about a million problems to work on, and Mary Anne was all ready for a long conversation about some boy I didn't even know!

"Don't you get it?" she said finally. "Lewis wants to meet you."

"That's silly," I said, sharpening a new pencil. "He doesn't even know me."

Mary Anne cleared her throat. "That's not exactly true. He, um, knows a *little* bit about you."

"How could he?" I was flipping through the book, trying to find my place when I paused and said, "Mary Anne, what have you done?"

She was blushing all the way up to her hair roots. "Now don't get annoyed, Dawn, but Logan and I told Lewis a few things about you. And I sent him a photograph of you."

"What?!"

"Please don't get upset. If you just think about it, you'll realize it was a great idea. Logan says Lewis is a really great boy, and I think he's just what you need just now." She was still clutching the white envelope and she handed it to me.

"It's a letter addressed to me," I said, turning it over. "Mary Anne, what's going on?"

"It's from Lewis. Isn't that great? He must have liked your photo and the things Logan and I told him, so he decided to write to you. I *said* he was a great guy."

"Terrific," I muttered, tearing open the envelope. I scanned the first few lines and relaxed a bit. Lewis said that he'd heard a lot about me, and he wanted to meet me. He also said I was very pretty and that we had a lot in common. He didn't sound too bad, but I just wasn't interested in meeting another boy at the moment. Why couldn't Mary Anne understand that?

"Well?" Mary Anne said. She stood next

to me, trying to read over my shoulder. "What do you think?"

I shrugged. "He seems like a pretty nice boy." A photo of a boy with dark brown hair and a nice smile fell out of the envelope. And he's even good-looking."

"Definitely. And he's a lot of fun, too. That's why Logan and I want this to work out." She looked at me very seriously. "You'll see him when he visits, won't you? *Please*, Dawn."

I looked at the photograph again. I didn't feel any sparks the way I had with Travis, but Lewis *did* seem nice. Still, the timing was wrong, all wrong.

"Well?" Mary Anne said impatiently. "Will you see him or won't you?"

I sighed. "I don't know."

"Dawn, puh-*leeze*!"

"Okay, okay. If Lewis wants to take me out when he comes to Stoneybrook, I'll go. I suppose."

"Good!" said Mary Anne. "That's all I wanted to hear."

15th CHAPTER

Later, when I was alone in my room, I read Lewis's letter again. (Okay, I'll tell you the truth. I read it *three* more times.) I'm not sure exactly what I was looking for, but I wondered if Lewis was too good to be true. He seemed funny, intelligent, not at all stuck-up, and *nice*. I'll show you what I mean. He started out by describing himself. (We had to do this once in an English lesson, and it was the toughest project I've ever had.)

DEAR DAWN,

I KNOW LOGAN IS GOING TO MAKE ME SOUND LIKE SOME FILM STAR, SO I THOUGHT ID SEND YOU MY PHOTO. THIS WAY YOU CAN MAKE UP YOUR OWN MIND. IM FIVE FOOT TEN, AND I HAVE BROWN EYES AND BROWN HAIR. NO MATTER WHAT LOGAN TELLS YOU, GIRLS DO NOT FAINT AT MY FEET.!

WAIT, I TAKE THAT BACK. A GIRL DID
FAINT AT MY FEET ONCE. HER NAME WAS
JENNY O'CONNOR. WE WERE DOING A
SCENE FROM A PLAY CALLED THE GLASS
MENAGERIE AND JENNY HAD THE WORST
CASE OF STAGE FRIGHT I'VE EVER SEEN. THE
CURTAIN WENT UP AND SHE PASSED OUT COLD!

SO MUCH FOR A BIG OPENING NIGHT. I
THOUGHT YOU MIGHT BE INTERESTED IN
ACTING, SINCE YOU'RE FROM THE WEST COAST.
WHENEVER I THINK OF CALIFORNIA, I
THINK OF FILM STARS AND HEALTH FOOD.
BUT I COULD BE WRONG. WHEN I TELL
PEOPLE THAT I'M FROM LOUISVILLE, THEY
ALWAYS THINK THAT I LOVE CHICKEN
AND THAT I HAVE A HOUND DOG NAMED
BEAU! (NEITHER IS TRUE.)

WELL, I BETTER WIND THINGS UP
HERE. I HOPE I HEAR FROM YOU!
'BYE FOR NOW.
LEWIS

Did I write back? Yes. But I took my
time, and I decided to be very casual.

Dear Lewis,
It was really nice to hear
from you. I can't believe that

118

Logan and Mary Anne sent you my photo! But you know what? I'm glad they did, because now we've met each other. (Sort of.)

I thought I'd start by telling you a little bit about myself. First of all, I love California, but not because it's full of film stars. In fact I've never even met a film star, even though a couple of them live near my dad.

You mentioned health food—I love it! Mum and I are always trying out new vegetarian recipes. (Don't gag. Spinach pie is delicious.)

Am I an actress? No way! People have always told me I should go into modelling or acting, but I know I'd get stage fright, just like your friend Jenny.

I'd like to tell you a little about Stoneybrook, but I have a maths test tomorrow

(panic time!) so I'd better go.
'Bye for now.
Dawn

I read my letter to Lewis twice before sealing the envelope. I wondered if I could have made it more interesting, decided that I couldn't, and finally dropped it in the postbox. Imagine how surprised I was when I got a letter back four days later! Lewis must have written the minute he'd received my letter.

DEAR DAWN,

THIS WILL HAVE TO BE SHORT, AS I HAVE A MATHS TEST, TOO. MATHS ISN'T MY BEST SUBJECT (ENGLISH IS) SO I HAVE TO STUDY EXTRA HARD. I'VE DONE ALL THE PROBLEMS IN THE BOOK THREE TIMES, SO UNLESS I TOTALLY FREAK OUT DURING THE TEST I'LL BE OKAY.

I LIKED HEARING ABOUT CALIFORNIA. I GUESSED THAT YOU WERE INTO HEALTH FOODS (ONE RIGHT ANSWER) AND THAT YOU WANTED TO BE AN ACTRESS (ONE WRONG ANSWER.) THAT GIVES ME A

SCORE OF FIFTY. LET'S HOPE I DO BETTER
ON THE TEST TOMORROW.
  SUPPOSE IT'S TIME TO HIT THE BOOKS.
I'M WONDERING WHAT KIND OF THINGS
WE CAN DO IN STONEYBROOK. A FILM?
A CONCERT? A WALK IN THE PARK?
          STAY IN TOUCH. YOUR PAL,
                        LEWIS

It sounded as if Lewis was planning to spend a lot of time with me when he visited Logan. Would it be just the two of us, or would we be doing things with Logan and Mary Anne? I decided I didn't really want to see him alone. That would be too much like a "date". But if he wanted to be friends, that would be okay.

Dear Lewis,
    I worked out what to do
when you visit Logan. How
about a tour of Stoneybrook?
I bet you've never seen a
small New England town. What
do we do for fun? We've got
cinemas and there's a big
shopping arcade, but you have
to drive to get to it. And of

121

course we have pizza parlours.
Do you know I found a place
that sells vegetarian pizza?
It has stir-fried snow peas
and broccoli on it, and it's
great!
                    your friend,
                        Dawn

In return, Lewis sent me a postcard of
Louisville, Kentucky. The picture was of a
beautiful boat called *The Belle of Louisville*,
and this was the message:

Hi, DAWN,

YOU'RE KIDDING ABOUT THE BROCCOLI PIZZA,
RIGHT? (PLEASE SAY YOU ARE!) I LIKE TO
TRY NEW THINGS, BUT THAT'S PUSHING IT A
LITTLE. STILL, IF YOU SAY IT'S GOOD, I'LL
TAKE YOUR WORD FOR IT. I'LL SEE YOU IN
STONEYBROOK SOON. I CAN'T WAIT TO
MEET YOU. I'M REALLY LOOKING FORWARD
TO IT.
                        'BYE, LEWIS

He was looking forward to coming to
Stoneybrook. He was looking forward to

seeing me. I read the postcard at least half a dozen times and put it in my notebook.

Mary Anne teased me just a little that night when I tucked the postcard into the mirror over my dressing table.

"So you're changing your mind a bit about Lewis?"

"He sounds . . . interesting," I said with a smile.

"Just interesting?"

"Okay, he sounds terrific." I paused. "But I don't want to get my hopes up too much. Remember how mad I was about Travis?"

"Lewis is different," Mary Anne said firmly. "Can't you tell from his letters?"

"I shrugged. "He seems different. He seems nice. And I don't think he wants to change me. We'll probably like each other. Just as friends," I added quickly.

"That's what I'm hoping for." Mary Anne sighed happily and flopped onto my bed. "I want you and Lewis to be great friends. Or maybe even something more," she said with a twinkle in her eye.

"Just friends will be fine."

Mary Anne giggled. "Only time will tell."